RHYTHMS OF RESISTANCE

GUYANA'S INDENTURED LEGACY

ABDUN NOOR

Vitasta

Published by
Renu Kaul Verma
Vitasta Publishing Pvt Ltd
4348/4C, Ansari Road, Daryaganj
New Delhi - 110002
info@vitastapublishing.com

ISBN: 978-81-988295-3-5

First Edition 2025

MRP ₹399

We gratefully acknowledge Project Gutenberg, for making this book possible.

Layout by Shubhpreet Kaur
Cover Design by Smriti Maheshwari
Printed by Chaman Enterprises, New Delhi

Ayla Noor Rajkumar
Kayvan Noor Rajkumar

One day in the future, your generation will perhaps read this socio-political fiction.
Perhaps a few of your generations, including yours, will find inspiration in your Grand Pa's narrative and undertake the quest to seek their respective roots, regardless of their nationality and language. They shall carry forward the traditional values and cultures of their ancestral societies to enrich their current motherland for the welfare of humanity across the globe.
I dedicate *Rhythms of Resistance,* articulating the maiden voyage of mythical Pegasus, to both of you and to your generation.

With blessings,
Nana Bhai

Contents

Prologue

In *Rhythms of Resistance*, my aim is to express the longing of the souls shackled far from their birth place. It unfolds the liberated spirits of those bound to servitude for three centuries, either as slaves or indentured workers in an unknown land named British Guiana. While majority of them came from India as indentured workers, others were forcefully procured from Africa to serve as slaves in the sugar plantations. Submitting to the brutal imperial greed of the colonial forces, all of them boarded ships grudgingly, and journeyed across seven seas and thirteen rivers to find shelter in this land.

Guyana's indentured legacy echoes the quest of Pegasus, the Greek mythical horse, yearning to soar the sky, struggles with the elusive art of flight despite possessing wings. My fiction draws its principal characters from the canvas of indentured workers migrating from India perhaps because I belong to this race and can relate this with my Bangla heritage.

My bond with the nation of Guyana, though brief, was far from fleeting. Shortly after my enlistment at the Headquarters of Washington, DC, my maiden mission took me to Guyana in September 1970. Thirteen long years passed before my next visit, in May 1983. Guyana, a country of eight million, graces the North Atlantic coast of South America. The proud Guyanese call it The Land of Six Races; five of which hail from distant shores—Indians, Africans, Portuguese, Chinese, and the British. The indigenous Amerindians are the natives.

Although a small nation, Guyana ascended the global arena starting from the early 1950s with its strong determined freedom movement. But a litany of engineered conflicts—strikes, riots, non-cooperation, dictatorship, electoral deceit, and factionalism among others—marred the nation's united spirit. Factions, colors, and political ideologies became the crucible of strife. It was not faith, but political beliefs that kindled these tumults. Communists, Marxists, Capitalists, and Socialists, all of them vied for political control over independent Guyana.

Skepticism loomed large; its roots traceable to Guyana's history. In 1807, the British Empire abolished slavery, a decree echoed in Guyana. This left British sugar plantations in Guyana bereft of laborers. To address this shortage, the British government introduced indentured laborers from India, Portugal, and China. However, most were of Indian origin. A staggering 238,960 Indian indentured laborers arrived in Guyana, with the majority departing from the port of Khidirpur, near Calcutta in Bengal, the then capital city of British India.

The story of *Rhythms of Resistance* transcends history, passing from one generation to the next through imagination, thought, and the enduring pain of the past. It is a narrative steeped in faith, where hatred, stigma, and suffering have silenced countless voices.

Earlier in 1987, I had sketched the legacy of Guyana's rebel hearts struggling for freedom from brutal British colonial forces in a Bengali socio-political fiction, *Pegasus*. My target audience was the restless youth in Bangladesh, either studying at the universities or entering the job market after graduation. The parents of this generation, under the leadership of Sheikh Mujibur Rahman, waged a liberation war in 1971 against the oppressive ruling military junta of Pakistan. In fact, the entire population of Bangladesh, 110 million people, participated in the liberation war, to make Bangladesh a free nation on 16 December 1971. But soon after the independence, a group of power-hungry, anti-liberation forces began a sustained campaign to divide the people, subvert the developmental progress and jeopardise the economic and political viability of the newly acquired independence. Collaborating with the armed forces, the anti-liberation political elements staged a coup d'état, and brutally assassinated the President,

Sheikh Mujibur Rahman, along with his entire family of eleven members (except two daughters studying abroad) on 15 August 1975.

The armed forces governed the country from 1975 onwards. The military dictatorship enabled a few families of nouveau riche to amass wealth at the costs of the underprivileged. The Bangladeshi youth became restless and demoralised. In contrast to the promises made by the leaders of the government leaders, opportunities of growth and advancement were limited. The dreams of the young generation were being shattered at every step of their innovative attempts due to engineered economic depression, unemployment, and increasing disparity between rural and urban areas. The nouveau riche class only consoled that harnessing economic development with equality between upper- and lower-income classes takes time. Frustrated, the youths questioned the very premises of a freedom which their parents have gained after sacrificing 3 million people. They questioned their own identity as a Bangladeshi, introspecting the very meaning of a hard-earned freedom.

I decided to bring to the forefront, the epic determination of Guyanese youth as a model for amelioratingtheidentitycrisisofmyprogenyinBangladesh. *Pegasus* was set in Guyana, during 1960 to 1964, when the populace of the struggling and impoverished colony experienced extreme violence, strikes and disruption of civil society. However, despite numerous provocations by external and internal forces, I found the young generation of the six races resolute in maintaining national unity. The collective voice of the youth, as forceful opinion makers, enabled independent Guyana to turn around the derailing economy and advance as a cohesive society.

I had written *Pegasus* 15 years after my first visit to Guyana during 1970. This fiction is entirely based on my impressions of the people of Guyana, drawing characters and mutual conversations from my imagination and recollecting places, such as neighbourhoods and streets, from my faded memories. If I have misspelled any names or sites, or offended someone, I offer my sincere apologies. *Pegasus* was a humble attempt to pay my tribute to the exemplary spirit of the youth of Guyana. I trust my current English rendition, *Rhythms of Resistance*, shall affirm my continuing tribute to the upcoming generation.

Chapter One

Slaughter House

On the rainy morning of 31 December 1964, Reeta Majeed, a sophomore at the prestigious Bishop's College in Georgetown, queued up for a part-time hairdresser position at the open entrance porch of the Clara Lodge, Georgetown. Reeta held her paper application close to her heart. The gentle sea breeze from the Seawall played with her freshly shampooed, long, black hair. Reeta noticed a small Tityra picking at its feed under the shade of a flamboyant flowering tree. The bird paused and eyed her directly with its sharp gaze. This was hardly a job of choice for Reeta. She could have easily retained the role of a gracious lady in an Indo-Guyanese aristocratic setting—indulging in opulent gatherings, leisurely moments, and overseeing household affairs by attendants. But, Reeta chose an unlikely path. What prevented her from claiming that crown is a startling story of destiny as her dream unfolds into a tragic tale.

***

On a September morning in 1963, Paromita, Reeta's mother, saw Mohon Singh devoutly offer a lighted candle at the Shiva temple just before sunrise, before departing for the Venezuelan border. She was impressed. Mohon Singh was a tall, handsome young man. His occupation as a pilot, manoeuvering aircrafts such as the DC-3 during World War II, brought both adventure and honour. It not only offered a substantial salary but also carried a pedigree of distinction within the social circles of Indo-Guyanese society. Such an illustrious profession, coupled with a prestigious lineage, made him a much sought-after bridegroom.

Lacking the courage to broach the matter with Reeta, Paromita left the task to her husband, Rehman Majeed. Reeta always listened to her father. Rehman too willingly agreed to discuss it with Reeta the next morning.

Rehman Majeed looked at the calendar. Time had passed quickly. Reeta was born just a while ago, it seemed. But the cruel calendar dictated that about 18 years had elapsed since her birth.

'Oh, Allah! It's already September 1963. She was born on 12 December 1945. My little Ammu will turn eighteen within three months. Paromita, we ought to celebrate her eighteenth birthday on a grand scale. We'll invite all her friends and our friends together,' Rehman Majeed exclaimed excitedly.

'Yes. This is about the time we should hold an

auspicious celebration for her within our society,' Paromita agreed in a serious tone. 'But, Rehman, it should not be a birthday party, but a wedding. Relatives and members of our *samaj* (society) are already gossiping about her delayed marriage.'

'Reeta is studying at Bishop's College. She is a serious student. I do not wish to thwart her higher education by tying her down with the iron shackles of family life. All this can wait till she finishes her graduation and is prepared to commence her professional career.'

'Marriage is destiny. Only the time is decided by God. However, it is our parental responsibility to start the process now, Rehman!'

'Yes, Paromita, our marriage was planned and organised by Allah Himself. We both grew up in the neighbourhoods of Georgetown; I spent 21 years, and you, 17. We both attended neighbouring schools. And yet, our first meeting took place in the faraway village of Ankerville, Port Mourant.'

'*Aji* Bachaoni invited *Maa* and *Baba* to attend the homecoming ceremony of *Nil Ankhi Bodhuji*, our blue-eyed bride. She insisted my parents to bring me along. Baba objected because I would miss school for a week. But *Aja* Jagan persisted that I should attend the welcoming ceremony organised for their son, Cheddi Jagan, and daughter-in-law, Janet Jagan. When necessary, I would act as an interpreter for Janet Jagan as she did not understand Bhojpuri.'

'It was Allah's plan. Aja Jagan ordered all the food items from our grocery store in Georgetown, especially the ones preferred by the *firangis*. Abba had loaded all the items in the delivery van and was to leave early in the morning, but he fell ill with a heart attack at midnight. Even from his sickbed Abba asked me to deliver the goods, starting for Ankerville before sunrise. I did not wish to leave him alone, but Amma insisted that I must fulfill the obligations Abba had made. It was my duty as the eldest son. That was the last time I saw my father. Abba returned to his Creator the next morning, at *subah sadiq* (dawn).'

'You were not informed of his death, Rehman. Maa said that if you had learned about his death, you would have rushed back to Georgetown from Aji Jagan's ceremony, thereby neglecting your duty.'

'Yes, Paromita. Sometimes, ignorance is bliss. For the rest of the seven days, we had a great time—stealing glances at each other, meeting under the mango tree when the rest of the family took their afternoon siesta, and at other odd times without the knowledge of either your parents, our hosts, or inquisitive relatives. Aji Bachaoni had planted so many fruit trees in her yard—guava, sapodilla, genip, sugar apple, banana, mango, and lots of vegetables for daily meals.'

'They were puritans. They ate nothing, but vegetables and *rotis*; they seldom ate rice. All those were grown in their backyards. The front yard had only colourful flowers.'

'And hiding behind the shady banyan tree, you ate all the guavas you could pluck. You even climbed the mango trees like a teenager,' Rehman chuckled with pride.

'It was not a banyan tree, my dear urban boy. And for your information, I was almost eighteen.'

'But you looked like thirteen!'

'You don't need to flatter me anymore now! I've grown old. My black hair is turning grey!'

'Age hasn't caught up with you, Paromita. You're as cheerful now as you were before.'

'But Rehman, you're no longer as adventurous as you were when we met. Perhaps, the business is weighing you down. You even took me on a trip to Aunty Annie Bethlyn's bakery in a nearby village in your delivery van. I was sitting next to you in the front seat. Each home had colourful flowers blooming on their porches. And the mutton patties from Aunty Annie's bakery were lovely! We almost got caught by Aunty Annie. Fortunately, you hid behind the van,' Paromita giggled.

'I had to whisk you out of the shop! Otherwise, rumours would have spread all over Guyana.'

'I was very cautious about my rendezvous with you.'

'But you dared to visit the Ankerville cricket ground with me on a lazy sunny afternoon, Paromita.'

'Why shouldn't I, Rehman? Cricket was your passion. You were a top spinner. You aspired to be a member of the Guyanese National Team.'

'But I had to leave all those passions to run the family business,' Rehman's voice reflected deep sorrow.

'You have rebuilt the family business. Your two younger brothers have completed their higher education. You have schooled your two sisters, and they are now happily married. I am proud of your accomplishments so far. But, we have a long way to go in the future by the grace of Allah,' Paromita encouraged Rehman.

'I still cherish the memories of Ankerville, the village where we fell in love with each other,' Rehman recalled.

'Yes, God plans creatively. We both grew up in neighbouring homes in Guyana for twenty years. We met in Ankerville before spending a lifelong journey together.'

'When we gain something, we also lose something, Paromita. I could not offer my prayers at the *Janaza* (Muslim funeral rights). I could not lay a *mutthi* (a handful of soil) to cover his *kobor* (grave). The material life of the eldest son prevented the spiritual duty of the eldest son.'

'Rehman, you have faithfully carried out your duty as the eldest son. I will perform *Pitra Puja* (worship the ancestors) for their souls. You will be rewarded, Rehman,' assured Paromita.

***

The next morning, Reeta was getting ready for college, raring to begin her first year of studies. She had excelled in English in her high school, which earned her a spot at the prestigious Bishop's College. Reeta hurriedly made her way out, carrying her bag on her shoulder, books close to her chest, and her skirt neatly arranged over her sandals. Her classes were starting in just two hours, and it was a brisk five-minute walk to Young Street. Once there, you'd catch a streetcar within a few minutes, taking you to the college campus for just a dollar. In all, it was a challenging journey of 20-25 minutes from home.

However, the real challenge was the early morning rush of hackney carriages coming in from Eteringbang, packed with commuters. Though they were essentially taxis, they operated like buses on specific routes, hence the name 'hackney carriages'. One could hop on and off anywhere along the route for the same flat fare—one Guyanese dollar.The real chaos erupted in the morning hours when folks from all over the land descended upon Georgetown. People from Annandale, Newtown Kitty, Bingil Ham, Amsterdam—they all filled the hackney carriages to the brim. Nobody was willing to get off at the Youngtown junction.

Yet, Reeta Majeed had her silver lining. Occasionally, her friend Siraj Sikdar would appear near the bus stop, his stylish Vespa parked beside Reeta. Offering him a fleeting smile, she would gracefully settle onto the back seat of the two-wheeler. Every day, she harboured the hope that Sikdar's Vespa would discreetly glide up beside her.

Engrossed in her tasks, she was softly humming to herself when an unexpected call from her Baba interrupted the tranquility. But he wasn't supposed to be home at this time. Managing a fleet of seven taxis, he catered to the transportation needs of the numerous foreigners in Georgetown. The escalating demands at Clara Lodge and other adjacent hotels for taxis, coupled with rising fuel costs due to the Jagan government's austere budget, kept Rehman Majeed on his toes every morning. Hence, Rehman Majeed almost always left home quite early in the morning. Reeta was surprised by his sudden appearance.

'Come on, Reeta, let me drive you to college,' he insisted. Reeta felt apprehensive. Her father was a reserved man; he had rarely made such offers in the past eighteen years.

She recalled the zoo excursion with her father about five years ago, when she was thirteen. Her mind was blossoming with evolving hues. As she beheld the dense clusters of fiery blossoms in the woodland, Reeta felt like the surging waves of youth colliding against the seawalls of Georgetown. The green leaves were just beginning to bloom with purple flowers.

'Don't you have any workload today, Baba? Won't you be heading to your business?' Reeta asked.

'Life isn't always about business, dear Ammu. Family matters are also important!' replied Rehman Majeed.

'You have left family management in Maa's

hands. Tell me, what family matters truly trigger your concern?' Reeta smiled.

'I have no idea how my life would have turned out if it weren't for her,' her father admitted.

'We all know that story. You both have spent twenty-five years together in your conjugal life. We grew up with one mother and one father. We haven't faced the pains of parental divorce. How many families in Guyana can claim that? How many Guyanese mothers have borne the burden of the family alone for so long? This would be your formal morning speech, Baba, wouldn't it?' Reeta jests at her father with a thin smile.

'Your maa,' Rehman Majeed interrupts proudly, 'She isn't Guyanese; she's an Indian girl born in Trivandrum. There's a difference in demeanour.'

'Let's not overstate the facts, Baba! In the end, we're all sons and daughters of India. We're all descendants of coolies,' Reeta replies.

'Everyone, except your mother. She comes from a very reputable household. About seventy years ago, her grandmother was an ally of Gandhi,' he explains.

Reeta had heard this story countless times, yet every time she heard it, her interest grew. The saga of a South Indian activist girl, falling in love with a handsome Guyanese man in Sabarmati Ashram, leaving the safe shelter of Mahatma Gandhi, traversing the seven seas and the thirteen rivers to arrive in Georgetown as an apostle of the famed sage, and embracing an exotic culture—this story intrigued her.

It sounded even better when Maa told the story of the rebellious Grandma. Reeta hadn't heard it in a while and longed to hear it again, like the tale of Cinderella. When she was a child, her mother would often tell her the story while braiding her black curly hair, her eyes and face gleaming.

'I need to sit with Maa tonight, and hugging her, I'll ask her to spin that story one more time. Maybe, Shovon will also join,' she mused.

'Enough with Maa's praises now,' Reeta exerted a mock scolding for her father. But Baba's words still resonated in her heart, a mix of pride and love lingering.

'Why are you suddenly giving me a lift at seven in the morning?' Reeta asked, but Rehman remained silent. He beckoned her to get inside the car, an old Vauxhall from 1945, still running well after 19 years, thanks to mechanic Raman Singh's craftsmanship. It had covered an impressive 250,000 miles, with many more to go. This aged taxi, still shining like new, stood out from the fate of other English taxis relegated to junkyards like antiques in their birthplace of colonial England.

The paramount virtue of an impoverished nation is its unwavering resilience—where people don't die until they die. Things endure, souls starved and limbs weary ultimately find rejuvenation through the skilled touch of capable hands.

'Reeta, have you pondered the path of your future life?' Baba asked, starting the car towards the college.

'I haven't finished college yet. Once I do, I will consider enrolling in medical school. What do you think, Baba?' Reeta replied.

'Why become a doctor?'

'Why, don't you know, Abba? My grandmother wanted to be a doctor but eventually ended up as a nurse in Georgetown. Ever since, I've dreamed of becoming a doctor,' Reeta, a bit irked, responded.

'Being a doctor is no small feat. Where will you go for your studies? Where is the college you might be admitted to?'

'Why? I'll study in Georgetown for two more years, and then I plan to go to Canada,' Reeta explained confidently.

'Have you thought about the cost? You'll have to pay $10,000 every year, for four straight years. Where will you get that huge amount from? Would we be able to afford such a large sum?' Rehman Majeed inquired.

'Don't worry about the expenses, Baba. I'm confident I'll secure a scholarship. Just support me for the first year, and I'll take care of the rest for the remaining years!' Reeta reassured.

'I wish I knew,' Rehman remarked, 'but what I hear from my Canadian clients is that competition in Canadian medical colleges is intense, and even

Canadian citizens find it challenging to enroll.'

'Don't overthink, Baba. Leave this challenge to me. There's no need to worry. If I can't make it to Canada, I'll go to the Dominican Republic. The costs are lower. I can finish the five years of study in just three and a half years. I'm determined to become a doctor,' Reeta declared.

Rehman had heard about the two medical colleges in Santo Domingo from many people, especially from his American clients. He had been probing for a long time, seeking a place where Reeta, a girl of Indian coolie descent in Guyana, could fulfill her dream of becoming a doctor.

Each of the clients he consulted, laughed. Never in Canada, America, or Britain, there wasn't a place for you folks in those schools. The competition is fierce, especially for Indian coolie girls.

'If she wants to study in the Caribbean Islands, there are only two possibilities, the Dominican Republic and Cuba,' Rodriguez advised.

Rehman had heard earlier that public medical colleges in Cuba are known not only for their excellent quality but also for their hospital facilities. Fidel Castro was willing to welcome students from the Third World. During one of his frequent visits to Guyana, Rodriguez had offered to secure a cultural exchange scholarship from the Ministry of Culture of Cuba for his daughter. Rodriguez had contacts with the concerned officials. Yet, Rehman had hesitated.

Rodriguez was the first client of his limousine business,

which started in 1949. Rehman Majeed had diligently carried on his father's delivery business for over five years after his death. By this period, his younger brother, Maatin Majeed had graduated from college with mediocre scores. Rehman decided to hand over the family trade to him. He bought a second hand limousine from a departing English businessman who decided to settle back in his cold homeland of England. Rehman Majeed ventured out, apparently for a lucrative limousine business. Guyana had emerged as a critical player on the geopolitical map of the Caribbean states following the ascension of Carlos Manuel as President of Cuba. Visitors from all over the globe, particularly from European countries, were descending upon Guyana in search of business and investment opportunities. The frequency of flights to Georgetown also increased.

The Timehri Airport, on the right bank of the Demerara River, was about 25 miles away from Georgetown. The roads to the airport were narrow, curvy, and occasionally treacherous. Midway was the bridge over the Demerara River. All types of vehicles crossed the bridge, often creating traffic hassles.

Rehman Majeed started after offering his *Fajr* prayers. Paromita stood beside the door with a glass of hot tea and a toast.

'May Mata Laxmi enable us to receive her blessings,' she prayed softly to her Goddess of Wealth.

Rehman Majeed had underestimated the time required to reach the airport. By the time he arrived, the KLM and BWIA flights had already landed, deboarded the Georgetown passengers, and taken off for the next stop, Caracas, the capital of Venezuela. It seemed most of the foreign passengers had completed their immigration and were on their way back to the capital city. Rehman was the only driver waiting for a passenger at the airport.

Rehman noticed a tall, lanky foreigner stepping out of the airport. He had no luggage! A small bag hung on his shoulder, and he was holding a long-wrapped item carefully. Perhaps it was a guitar. He looked and walked just like Nat King Cole. He walked down the aisle to the limousine stand.

'I'm looking for a cab. Are you available?' he asked with a distinct nasal tone.

Rehman nodded and opened the bonnet of his car.

'Allow me to load your luggage!'

'This isn't luggage. This is my guitar. Could I rest it on your back seat?'

'This car is small. There may not be enough space for both you and the guitar.'

'Usually, I prefer to sit in the front seat. Would you have any objection?' he asked politely.

'It's your preference. In our business, the client is always right. Please be seated!' Rehman opened the front door.

Rehman Majeed started the engine.

'I'm sorry for my ill manners. I haven't yet introduced myself,' he said, extending his hand to Rehman.

'Neither have I introduced myself. I'm Rehman Majeed, and this is my car.'

'I'm Rodriguez. I'm coming from Florida. I'm a musician, I play the guitar.'

'I presumed so! You're indeed dressed like Nat King Cole and walk like Nat King Cole,' Rehman said, feeling at ease with his first client.

'I'm flattered, Rehman. I hope you won't mind if I address you as Rehman. Indeed, Nat is my idol.'

'Are you visiting Guyana for a performance? Where is your entourage? Or, is it a solo act? Usually, concerts take place at Cinema Metropole.'

'I play guitar and sing for myself. I don't perform for an audience,' Rodriguez stated with a sudden grim tone and fell silent for a while.

Rehman began his drive to Georgetown. The visitor remained silent, lost in deep thoughts. Rehman didn't wish to break his deep introspection. All visitors stayed in any of the five moderately priced hotels in Georgetown, all within a five-mile radius. As he neared downtown, he would ask Rodriguez for his hotel's address.

About 45 minutes passed without a word between them. Rodriguez, wearing a pair of sunglasses, kept looking outside, left, right, and front, with deep attention. They crossed the bridge of the Demerara River. Rodriguez started humming, his mood changing.

'Where will you be staying? We'll be reaching downtown in about 30 minutes,' Rehman decided to ask at this point. 'Or, will you be travelling to the interior coasts? In that case, we'll be reaching the intersection within 10 minutes.'

'Oh, I'm so sorry, I didn't tell you my destination. After the sudden death of my father, I've become very moody. My mood changes frequently, like the colour of a sky full of floating dark clouds! Please, allow me to extend my apologies to you!' Rodriguez was sincerely apologetic.

'I understand your sorrows, Rodriguez. My father also left me suddenly. I've also gone through phases of agony like you,' Rehman sympathised.

'Could you please take me to Clara Lodge?'

Rehman abruptly placed his foot on the brake and turned to Rodriguez.

'Do you mean the Clara Lodge?'

'Yes! Clara Lodge. The Lodge is actually a few blocks away from downtown.'

'I know. We'll be at the Lodge within 15 minutes.'

Rehman wondered whether he should broach his concern. Clara Lodge was a century-old classic hotel in Guyana. It was very expensive; only the rich and privileged were privy to the Lodge. During the past hundred years, kings and queens, Presidents and Prime Ministers had graced the Lodge by staying there.

Rodriguez was his first client. Should he tell him this? He decided to dodge the topic.

They entered the entry porch of Clara Lodge. A turbaned bellboy of Indian origin rushed out of the door to collect the baggage.

Rodriguez opened up his wallet.

'I forgot to ask you the fare earlier. I'm presuming you'll charge me the correct amount. May I pay you in US dollars?' He flashed the green currency. 'Or, shall I exchange the currency for you at the Lodge reception?'

'Whatever you prefer!' Rehman answered and stated the desired fare.

'Will you be available to take me around Georgetown, Rehman?' Rodriguez asked.

'Meeting the needs of visitors is my business, Rodriguez,' Rehman smiled.

'I usually rent a car with a driver for a full day, at least for 12 hours, if not more! And I make my contract for the entire period of my stay. If you're willing, I can offer you a contract for the period of my stay in Georgetown, 14 days from today.'

Rehman appeared amazed by the offer. Paromita's prayers were being answered by Maa Laxmi.

'I can pay you in advance for the first week now.' Rodriguez opened his wallet again.

'Your words are my advance, Rodriguez. When should I report for my new contract?'

'I had an all-night flight from Miami. I need to rest. Your contract begins at 9 am tomorrow. Have a good day.'

Rodriguez entered the doors of the Clara Lodge, which the Indo-Guyanese bellboy was patiently holding.

Rehman rushed back home to convey the good news to Paromita.

The next morning, Rehman Majeed arrived at the driveway of Clara Lodge sharp at 9 am. Rodriguez was waiting, adorned in a British-style safari outfit with a straw hat on his head. He walked slowly and steadily, in a style reminiscent of Nat King Cole, towards the waiting car. He wasn't carrying his guitar.

'I would like to meet Dr Janet. I assume you know her whereabouts?' Rodriguez asked.

Rehman was taken aback.

'Do you mean Dr Janet Cheddi Jagan, the wife of the dental surgeon Dr Cheddi Jagan? Do you have a dental problem? Both of them have a clinic downtown. Their office hours are 9:30 am-5:30 pm. We could be the first clients, waiting without an appointment.'

'No, I'm not having any dental problems. I wish to meet the couple and congratulate them personally on their wedding.'

'The wedding happened six years ago, in 1943. I attended it!' Rehman exclaimed.

'I wrote a letter of congratulations at that time, but it wasn't answered. Perhaps, I had the wrong postal address.

Janet was my classmate at Wayne State School. But I didn't meet Cheddi during those times.'

'I understand, Cheddi was very busy studying in America, earning his tuition fees and livelihood. He hardly had any time to socialise.'

'Life as an undergraduate student in the USA is tough, especially for those who have to work to meet the high tuition fees. I know; I worked too. At that time, there was no student loan scheme. Either your parents paid for your higher education, or you had to meet your aspirations on your own. There was no support from the public treasury.'

'Cheddi engaged in several odd jobs, the kind that whites didn't want to do, and even the blacks despised.'

'Life is tough for coloured students wherever you go for studies—the USA, Canada, England, or the Netherlands,' Rodriguez commented.

'We've reached High Street. This is their office. The door has just opened. Janet will be thrilled to meet you after so many years!' Rehman remarked.

Rodriguez got out of the front seat of the car.

'I'll be waiting in the parking lot. Take your time!'

Rehman moved his car to the parking lot. He waited for more than two hours. Rodriguez walked out of the office, smiling.

'Janet was excited. Cheddi was very courteous and hospitable,' Rodriguez commented.

'The couple commands tremendous admiration from

the common people of Guyana,' Rehman said proudly.

'I'm so privileged, Rehman. Both of them briefed me on what they intend to do to uplift the economic life of disadvantaged Guyanese in the interior. They talked about their dreams of forming and organising workers' cooperatives and improving the health conditions of expecting mothers in the sugar plantations. I volunteered my expertise to them.'

'Have you been involved with cooperatives?' Rehman asked.

'Not yet! But I was involved with labour unions. I'll learn!' Rodriguez admitted.

Over the next few days, they criss-crossed Guyana from east coast to west coast, from north to south. They drove to remote villages and towns, meeting grassroots communities of all races. They visited plantations, factories, mills, and the paddy fields of young entrepreneurs and rice farmers introducing new breeds of rice. They stayed in small inns and rest places. It was an unforgettable experience for Rehman. The more Rehman, the urban child of Georgetown, toured the interiors of his own country, the more he loved the people of all six races equally. It was an eye-opener.

'I would like to meet Forbes. Could this be arranged, Rehman?' Rodriguez asked the night before his departure from Georgetown.

'You mean, our dashing barrister? Forbes returned home a couple of years ago after completing his Bar at

Law at Gray's Inn. He has started his law practice, and it's booming. But, unlike other lawyers, Forbes doesn't take any fees from relatively poor clients.'

'Yes, Forbes Burnham. If possible, I'd like to pay my respects to him before I leave for the USA.'

'Forbes was a brilliant student. He was awarded the British Guyana Scholarship as the top student from Guyana at the University of London.'

'I didn't know Forbes was such a meritorious student,' Rodriguez exclaimed, surprised.

'His father, James Burnham, was a scholar! He was the head teacher of Kitty Methodist School. He taught for more than 25 years. His home fostered scholarship. Jessie, his daughter, was also a brilliant student. I knew her. They lived at 4, Pike Street,' Rehman narrated with great admiration for the Burnham family.

The next morning, Rehman drove Rodriguez to the chambers of Barrister Forbes Burnham. As usual, he waited for him, parking his car on the street. Private schools were about to open; they started earlier than public schools. Young teenagers, clad in school uniforms, were rushing to school. Rehman dreamed that one day, his son, Shovon, and daughter Reeta would also be enrolled in those prestigious private schools. Whatever high tuition fees were required, Rehman would earn that through his limousine business. The start of the limousine business had already bestowed upon him abundant livelihood, much like a *rizq* (provision) from Allah.

'He's a remarkable lawyer,' Rodriguez startled the daydreaming Rehman with his comment as he opened the front door of the car.

'One day, Forbes will become a great political leader of Guyana. Cheddi and Forbes will bring significant changes to Guyana. Maybe, one day, they'll even march hand in hand for the freedom of Guyana!' Rodriguez asserted.

Rehman drove directly to the airport. The flight to Miami was scheduled for 2 pm.

Rodriguez embraced Rehman as he bid farewell to his first client.

'I have fallen in love with Guyana. I'll try my best to advance the cause of the people of Guyana,' murmured Rodriguez. 'I'll return to Georgetown.'

'When, Rodriguez?' asked an emotional Rehman, not to his first client, but his first firangi friend.

'I don't know when, Rehman, but I shall return. And when I return, I'll seek you out for my rides.'

Rodriguez picked up his guitar from the back seat and slowly walked to the airport door, without glancing at Rehman waiting in the driveway.

Rodriguez was an oddball. Over the next decade, he frequented Georgetown, sometimes staying for weeks, sometimes for months, and occasionally just overnight. Whenever Rodriguez arrived, Rehman barely had time to catch his breath. Rodriguez would immediately seek out the same limousine upon arrival in Georgetown, booking it throughout the day and night. Despite Rehman's pride in being a self-made millionaire, Rodriguez insisted on having him as his chauffeur. They travelled many places together—making midnight visits, attending strange parties with people of diverse races, and listening to various community leaders. Rehman silently observed Rodriguez, his client and friend for 14 years, unable either to love him or let him go.

***

'Studying isn't everything in life; you need to think about starting a family too,' Rehman said, startling Reeta, as this was a question her father had never asked her.

'Why the rush to marry me off? Do you see me as a financial burden?' Reeta asked.

'Reeta, starting a family when you find a good boy might be a better option for your future than just studying,' Rehman replied, his voice muffled.

'Are you going to prioritise having grandkids over the education of your only daughter, Abbu?' Reeta asked, her eyes wide open.

Sensing sarcasm, Rehman became agitated. 'You've studied a lot as a coolie's daughter. Now you wish to make a career as a doctor, like an independent, unmarried white lady? A coolie's daughter should remain a coolie.'

Reeta grew uneasy. His tone wasn't typical of Rehman. Understanding him this morning proved elusive.

'Oh, Baba! Won't you tell me the name of the handsome boy you've selected?' Reeta asked in a soft voice.

'I haven't selected anyone, Reeta. Your Maa has chosen a boy. I trust your Maa's choice.'

'Baba, you're still keeping me in suspense!' Reeta exclaimed, touching her father's shoulder affectionately.

'Pilot Mohon Singh,' Rehman replied, 'the one who flies his DC-3 to Kurakula every morning.'

'Oh, that lad who used to be my playmate in childhood. Doesn't he have a dark, I mean, really dark complexion? He doesn't quite seem Indian, does he?' Reeta giggled.

Reeta had a point. She was fair-skinned and wouldn't really match Mohon's darker complexion.

Rehman felt fury surge inside him as soon as he heard Reeta's remarks. So, now she aspired to climb the steep ladder of Guyana's mixed colonial society! But she didn't realise that those with dark skin would never ascend to such heights within Guyanese social scales. God himself had preordained glory for the Caucasian; one must possess the complexion of a white horse.

In the throes of fury, Rehman found himself mumbling, his bizarre habit of expressing discontentment. In moments of anger, Rehman clung to these grumbles, expressing the storm brewing within. Echoes of their shared history resonated in his mind. In Paromita's absence, his fury intensified, engulfing the entire family like a whirlwind. No matter how heavy the workload, Paromita had to pacify the raging Baba.

A shiver of terror ran down Reeta's spine.

***

Painful memories of the past, passed down through generations of Indo-Guyanese descendants, reminded Rehman of the conduct of his forefathers. When the British recruited his great-grandfather Syed Lutful Majeed from Calcutta, they didn't care about his lineage, whether he hailed from the esteemed Syed family or was a low-caste coolie's or a scavenger's son. The British agents, paid to recruit indentured workers from impoverished villages, were tasked only with scrutinising the age, appearance, and physical abilities of prospective workers, not the colour of their skin. Once spotted as a potential recruit, a vast net, woven by multiple conspirators, was cast, dragging every prospect to the bustling docks of Khidirpur, a seaport of Bengal. For about a century and a half, caravans of ships sailed from this port towards the new lands of the Caribbean.

A gripping scandal unfolded, shrouded in darkness. The narrative seeped into the family of Rehman Majeed through hushed murmurs and entwined with the family of Konoval Singh. It penetrated every nook of fragmented Indo-Guyanese households, embedding itself in their shared imagination. They, in turn, reshaped and embellished the tale within their minds. What significance did colour, caste, or race hold on that particular day?

Rehman Majeed recalled the days of his great-grandfather, Syed Lutful Majeed. It was 1844. He was a youth, rebelling against British colonial rule in Bengal. Despite his father's illustrious Syed lineage, poverty overshadowed their lives. The prospect of funding his higher education after graduating from secondary school with high marks posed a financial challenge to the family.

One day, Syed Lutful Majeed spotted a British near their home, conversing with his father. His father summoned Lutful and introduced him to the man.

'His name is Johnson. He is a Sahib from London. He will return within a week with a job offer for you. Don't forget to accompany him.'

'What type of job and where?' inquired Lutful.

'You'll understand when Sahib returns and takes you to the town of the job,' his father replied. Without exchanging further words, his father prepared for *wudu*, the ritual washing of hands, face, and feet before Islamic prayers. He then proceeded to the nearby mosque for the evening prayers as the sun began to set.

'And, don't forget to take my sword with you!' his father shouted back while washing his left foot.

'What's the point of taking your sword with me to

my job town?' Lutful Majeed argued. 'Following our family tradition, my grandfather handed it over to you during your wedding as the eldest son. It's a symbol of your union.'

'It'll prove to be a useful symbol for your future life. Always keep it close to yourself and within your own family. Hand it over for safekeeping only to your eldest son and ask him to carry out the same practice for the next generation. The traditions of our Syed family mandate that this sword should be given only to the eldest male member of successive generations of Syed lineage!' his father dictated.

Leaving a befuddled Lutful at the steps of the pond of their ancestral home, his father headed off to say his *Maghrib* (evening) prayer. Little did Lutful know that this was their final farewell.

Three days later, Sahib Johnson returned to the village, bringing a horse-drawn carriage with a *sais (horse caretaker)*. He asked Lutful to ride in the carriage. The two horses galloped forward under the command of the sais. Sahib came inside and sat beside an apprehensive Lutful Majeed, who was dressed in traditional Muslim attire, white kurta and pajama, clutching his father's wedding sword wrapped in a shiny red muslin cloth.

'Will you be carrying that with you during your long journey?' Sahib inquired, a smile playing on his lips.

'Dad asked me to always keep it with me,' Lutful

replied in a hushed tone.

'Very well! It's nice to retain a heritage from your homeland,' Mr Johnson chuckled.

Lutful failed to appreciate the long-lasting effects of those words until it was too late. By the time he realised it, the ship *Davenport* had disembarked from Khidirpur dock and set sail for the seven seas and thirteen rivers.

The horses tirelessly galloped throughout the night. Johnson Sahib, Lutful Majeed, and the sais stayed up all night. They arrived at Khidirpur dock just before sunrise.

Lutful Majeed was surprised. It looked as if an entire market had gathered, around four hundred men and a handful of women, perhaps twenty or twenty-five in total. Their attire varied, some were in dhotis, others in *Panjabis*, some in trousers, and a few in their *nengtis*. All the girls, however, were adorned in sarees.

The crowd was a mix, with a few looking intelligent and inquisitive, while the majority appeared very miserable. Each face bore either the impression of confronting a challenging world or the glow of a shadowed void. It was a rare sight for Lutful to witness so many adult men and women belonging to different castes, creeds, colours, and faiths, gathered in one place, their eyes filled with a mix of wonder, apprehension, and fear!

'Fall in and board the ship. Boys go first, followed by girls. Maintain your cool,' a hoarse command suddenly rang out from an unseen commander. But hardly anyone heeded the call immediately. A handful climbed the steps to the ship hesitantly, while others lingered. Gradually, most of them boarded the ship, gazing ahead with frightful anticipation. The final few were dragged up to the dock.

Grinning, Sahib Johnson finally entered the ship. He handed out a rectangular white sheet of paper to each person in the waiting crowd. The shorter men squatted on the ship's open deck. The older men encircled them, while the weaker women took positions in the centre, resembling the beads of a necklace.

'Please read and sign. Each one of you! If you can't write, use your thumb impression,' Johnson stated in a dictatorial tone.

The gathered men and women exchanged curious glances. What was written on the white paper? Why were they being asked to sign? Lutful Majeed's mind swelled with unknown thoughts, but no one dared to ask. Instead, they scrutinised each other's faces, their questions growing larger in the lines of their eyes and mouths. Mr Johnson broke the silence.

'I understand you are curious to know what has been written on this single page of white paper. This is a formal letter of agreement between you and the British Raj. This document outlines your obligation to serve the British Raj, who has enlisted you for an initial period of five years. After completing this term, you are free to enter into another five-year contract. After a decade of service, the

British Raj will cover the expenses of your return home. Your participation in this is entirely voluntary, as all of you are over the age of eighteen. With your full consent, you have embarked on this ship, fully obliged to your word of faithfully serving the British Raj.'

These words struck them all like a bolt of lightning, swelling their eyes and ears with surprise. It was a peculiar employment arrangement, unheard of and unknown, revealing an unfamiliar job offer.

'We have secured your employment with the full consent of either your parent or legal guardian. I assure you that after completing the job, each of you will return to your motherland, India. We are committed to sending you back to this Bengal port,' Sahib continued.

This time, Lutful was even more stunned. Anguish and anger welled within him. His father knew, he had given consent for the upcoming journey. But he had no courage to inform Lutful personally.

Sahib's words seemed endless. He continued, 'We have provided your guardians five hundred tonka in advance for each of you. Some may invest in land; others may start a small business. You have entered the service of the British Raj for the happiness and eventual prosperity of your families back home, and to enhance the quality of your lives abroad. You may note that the salaries for the first two years of your service have already been advanced to your respective families. Therefore, you will start receiving your cash salary from the beginning of the third year.'

Questions swirled within Lutful's mind: Where will I go? Why this sea journey? What job awaits me? The inquiries clustered in his throat. Yet, he observed that everyone was silent, as if rendered mute by these unforeseen developments. Countless faces bore a blank, feeble expression, with only their eyes radiating a painful glow. However, no words escaped their lips.

Lutful gingerly raised his hand and gently inscribed his name, Syed Lutful Majeed, in Roman letters on the white paper he held. After all, he was literate! The signature in English did not escape the notice of Sahib Johnson.

The journey commenced on the ship *Davenport* in March of 1844.

***

A parallel and similar narrative unfolded for about 144 Indians on that fateful morning of 1844. They lined up similarly, boarding the ship *Davenport* one by one, embarking on a journey to an unknown land, and thus initiating a new odyssey towards an exotic destination. Although each one's story and memories are unique, a shared thread weaves them together—the thread of deprivation, falsehood, stifled pride, and treachery by their own kin. The tales of yesteryears echo through many mouths, their colours changing, and words evolving, yet the essence remains the same.

Pratima, the great-grandmother of Mohon Singh, held a different but equally distinctive tale. Pratima's recollections narrate another personal story of family betrayal. It all happened on a decisive day when she accompanied her grandmother to the temple for a widow's offering. The details of her childhood marriage and the playful exchange of garlands had long faded from her memory. Likewise, the day her husband departed from this world was shrouded in oblivion. Yet, the peculiar rules of the Brahmin samaj dictated that she should continue to live as a widow and pay monthly homage at the temple to free the bonded *atma*, the soul of her departed husband.

Holding on to her grandmother's little finger, Pratima stepped into Calcutta. The temple was unfamiliar to her. This time, her grandmother, more acquainted, led her to the temple to make offerings for her husband, herself, and for the regular prayers. Moments later, she discovered her grandmother conversing with a British gentleman near the temple. Pratima noticed the sahib's brown eyes, red hair, and unattractive appearance. The sahib cast frequent glances at her. Pratima, unable to focus on the idols or make her offerings, kept stealing glances at the sahib, growing increasingly bashful, and pulling the *anchal* of her white saree over her bosom.

After completing her conversation in a soft voice, Grandma came up the stairs and beckoned Pratima to follow her. Sahib was eagerly waiting atop the slippery temple stairs. Looking at the sahib, Grandma smiled and winked. Then, with a twinkle in her eye, she said, 'Pratima, come here! This is our firangi sahib. He came to see our temple. I have shown him around. Now, please show him the way out of this sacred temple.'

'Oh, as if the sahib doesn't know the way! Granny, if you want to lead the way so much for the gentleman, be my guest,' Pratima retorted sarcastically.

'Pratima, we have already incurred a sin by bringing him within the boundaries of our sacred *mandir*. While returning, the sahib's path might be evasive. He may decide to stay back within the temple premises. We must not incur further sin. You should guide him out with your candlelight. Otherwise, he might stray from the return path,' Grandma insisted.

The sahib did not stray, but Pratima indeed strayed from her miserable life without her consent. Once outside the temple, the sahib drew near, firmly grasped her trembling hands, and dragged her onto the ship after a while. Everytime Pratima closed her eyes, she saw that cunning smile on her grandmother's lips and the glint of intrigue in her eyes.

'Didn't the British strip us of our rights? Didn't Bukra lie?' Rehman yelled, trembling with rage. 'We've been imprisoned by the caste, robbed by our kin—our fathers, mothers, grandmothers, and relatives. We're astute; deceit is our craft.'

Rehman dropped Reeta in front of the closed iron gate of Bishop's College with a silent goodbye and proceeded to the depot to manage his rental fleet.

***

A few lazy weeks in September of 1963 pass by. One day, as Reeta came out of Bishop's College, she finds Mohon Singh patiently waiting for her. Why has Mohon come, and when did he arrive? Reeta wonders as she approaches him. A couple of weeks have elapsed since her conversation with Baba, and in the meantime, Maa has had a few chats with her.

'Let's go to Kaieteur Falls,' Mohon Singh requests directly, without any pretense.

'Where on earth is that falls?' Reeta asks, her eyes wide with surprise and her lips softly parted.

'Right down the picturesque estuary of the Potaro River, near the Venezuelan border,' Mohon replies.

'Way out there! How are we going to get there? How long will it take?' Reeta pretends to be surprised as her eyes glowing with mock deceit.

'We'll leave early and return by evening. There's no reason to stay the night with me,' Mohon Singh laughs, sensing her uneasiness about the trip.

'I'm not that easy,' Reeta flirts cynically.

'We'll test those words later,' Mohon winks. 'Be ready

at five in the morning.'

True to his word, Mohon Singh arrives before dawn, driving his father's old Volkswagen. As they stand before 117, Water Street—Reeta's home—they begin, perhaps, to turn the page to the next chapter of their lives.

It's Reeta's first time on a plane, and that too in the cockpit with the pilot. The thrill is different. It is a small airport with a short runway. A plane is parked near the runway. Next to the plane, about twenty passengers are waiting, mostly middle-aged Indians working as rice farmers in the estuary of the Mazaruni River. Piles of jute sacks filled with potatoes and sugar are stacked next to the passengers.

Mohon Singh, donning a pair of dark sunglasses, inspects each waiting passenger and surveys the loads. He asks the porters scrambling with the sacks to load them quickly. He looks at the clouds and the disappearing stars. The sun will soon rise. He asks the passengers to board the plane quickly.

Finally, Mohon turns to Reeta, who had felt ignored until then.

'It's our turn to board the plane, Reeta,' Mohon invites with a grin. Reeta climbs the short steps of the plane, noticing that it is half-empty with many seats removed, and the porters still scrambling with the sacks. Within a few minutes, the porters leave the plane. Mohon boards, followed by Amoz Rangeela, his so-called flight navigator.

Mohon Singh signals Amoz Rangeela to close the front door, and starts the engine.

'The door latch doesn't feel right, Pilot,' shouts Amoz Rangeela. Despite his repeated attempts, he fails to close the front door. 'The door won't shut, Pilot! What should I do now?' Amoz asks.

'Ah, darn it! Give it a strong pull and then a good shove. This thing never cooperates even when I'm in a good mood!' Mohon Singh curses.

Shocked, Reeta asks, 'Who are you cursing this early in the morning?'

'It's the plane, not Amoz. I wish it behaved properly when I'm expected to be in a good mood,' Mohon smiles. Suddenly, a single pull causes the back door latch to disengage from its hinge, closing the interior of the plane.

'Prepare for take-off, Pilot. The sky is clear and the weather favourable, no clouds in sight, a direct path ahead,' Amoz Rangeela instructs.

Mohon starts the engine, but it doesn't ignite. He launches into another round of vehement curses, exclaiming, 'Damn you, you scoundrel!'

Mohon's persistent cursing seems to have finally reached the heart of the DC-3. The engine struggles to come to life for a few minutes, strives to warm up, but then abruptly shuts down.

'This thing is cursed today. She's seeking blood, red blood,' Mohon Singh erupts into another bout of expletives, then abruptly shifts to a more polite tone. 'Sorry, Reeta, for my ill manners. This plane refuses to take-off without a proper scolding. She has a troublesome, arrogant ego, constantly in need of reprimanding.'

As Mohon Singh forcefully clicked the key again, the engine roared furiously, holding back its apparent anger.

Reeta felt that the heart of the plane, the engine, throbbing, just like her own heart, which was as nervous as a white dove. She was certain that the engine possessed a living soul. Realising that Reeta understood its agonies, the engine, still shaking with jealousy, urged its two propellers to rotate vigorously. The wind causes Reeta's freshly shampooed hair to flutter. Instantly, the DC-3 lurches forward like a boar, then swiftly ascends into the sky.

Reeta sensed that as they scaled the heights, the once haughty DC-3 transformed into a graceful bird, exuding an air of joy. A mix of fear and excitement coursed through her. Gradually, the scenery below shrinks, trees, people, and cars become mere dots. Eventually, only vast green landscapes remains—solitary trees, hills, and valleys.

Reeta floats with a surge of joy as the DC-3 chases clouds like tufts of cotton. Below, a velvety expanse of green resembles a worshipful carpet. In the cockpit, Mohon Singh, now a determined man with no repertoire of curses, hums as the grudging engine roared on softly, emitting an aura of envy.

'Are you feeling great, Reeta?' Mohon Singh's stern

expression suddenly turned polite and cordial. 'We've climbed to 13,000 feet. Now, she'll fly smoothly.'

Mohon Singh released the steering wheel, reaching to touch Reeta's dark hair. Reeta grips her shaking long fingers tightly. Mohon Singh catches a whiff of Reeta's perfume. Suddenly, the engine rumbles once again, and the left propeller slows down. The DC-3 abruptly tilts to the left, causing Reeta to stumble onto Mohon Singh.

Mohon Singh gently pushes Reeta back into her seat with a firm hand and exclaims, 'Tighten your belt, Reeta. We're hitting unusual air turbulence. The control tower never warned us about these air gaps.'

'Why are you staring at us in the cockpit?' Mohon Singh scolds Amoz Rangeela with a hot temper. 'Instead, ask everyone to move to the left. We need to regain balance.'

However, there was no time to balance; all the sacks of wheat and potatoes had already shifted to the right. Reeta observes the plane descending rapidly.

Reeta screams in terror, 'Mohon, Mohon, take control of your plane. We're going down! Look, look!'

'This plane will never go down. She knows how to protect herself. There's nothing to worry about as long as the loads on the right and left sides are balanced,' Mohon laughs heartily, his face gleaming with innocence.

By then, everyone had shifted to the left and resettled. The plane still leans slightly to the right, although the humming noise has diminished. 'We need to move more sacks manually,' Mohon yells. Amoz Rangeela silently moves towards the rear end.

Summoning a few other passengers, including two robust boys, he calls for assistance. Together, they move the sacks to the left. Gradually, the plane gains altitude. Its attitude improves. The buzzer goes off, and it resumes with a soft hum.

Breathing a sigh of relief, Mohon asks, 'How do you feel now, Reeta?'

Reeta admired Mohon Singh's flying skills and his fearlessness under stress. Without saying a word, she just rolls her eyes and smiles quietly.

'Look down, Reeta! We're now at the estuary of the Mazaruni River. That's where we'll land.'

'Land? In the middle of nowhere? Surrounded by woods and trees? Where's the airport?' Reeta shares her concern.

Mohon Singh chuckles, breaking his usual reserve. This time, his hearty laugh made Reeta feel that he was her strongest, best friend.

'Do you think the Cheddi-Forbes duo would bother building an airport for a handful of Indian rice growers? Come on, that's just wishful thinking. It's different even with the blacks! The Indians are born paupers. But in our mixed kingdom, even enduring poverty is a luxury for the poor of each race.'

'How will you land the plane?' Reeta inquires.

'There's a strip of open ground for grazing down there.

That's where we'll touch down, by the river,' Mohon reassures her.

The DC-3 swoops down like a hawk, making a dramatic entrance even before Mohon finished speaking. The plane rushes down the gravel-covered road running parallel to the riverbank.

A bunch of hungry-looking children and a flock of old folks come running towards the plane even before the engine stopped. Though dressed modestly, it is evident that all of them were Indian. In these areas, they sow rice and thresh it.

All the passengers, except four, disembark, carrying the fat-bellied sacks. The plane emptied within fifteen minutes. Checking her wristwatch, Reeta notes it was barely 9.30 am. She assumed Mohon Singh's work was complete and that his voice would be much softer this time. On their first date, Reeta didn't quite appreciate Mohon teasing his associate and hurling abuses on the DC-3 plane.

'Amoz, get ready quickly,' Mohon Singh announces, and walks slowly towards Reeta. He says softly, 'Reeta, it's time for our actual trip to begin, to Kaieteur Falls, near the Venezuelan border. I'll treat you to lunch there.'

'What? Are we not done already?'

'Of course not. This was just a warm-up. Our next destination is Kaieteur Falls. It should take an hour and a half. I'll serve you lunch there, and on the way back, I'll fly directly to Georgetown. We'll be back just in time for your classes to end,' Mohon says with a mischievous smile. 'I promise, no one will ever know about our secret rendezvous!'

'What's in it for us?' Reeta sounded a bit annoyed.

'You'll see once we arrive. Besides, shouldn't they reach their hometown too?'

Reeta glanced over her shoulder and saw four Amerindians huddled together inside the plane. She reflected silently. Must Mohon fly another two hours for those Amerindians? Why not ask Mohon to return to Georgetown now? They could head to the park from the airport, sit in the shade of Gulmohar, have *aloo bhaji* and *paratha*, and chat about all the childhood stories, like playing *Ekka Dokka* (hopscotch).

'Oh no, not really,' Mohon Singh insisted. 'They're just a warm-up. The real gem awaits you once we reach our destination.'

'Gem? Why not tell me what it is right away?' Reeta's voice sweetened.

'Patience, Reeta, patience,' Mohon Singh maintained his suspense. He then leaped into the cockpit, and after a while, they took–off into the air.

Reeta wondered if Mohon Singh was antisocial. Why did sitting in the cockpit always require him to either curse his plane or silently murmur his thoughts? Did Mohon remain engulfed in the anxieties and pressures of the world even while flying? she wondered.

Slumber overtook Reeta, though she didn't know when. By the time she woke up, a thick circle of darkness had enveloped them. The sky was inky, covered in a thick layer of black cotton. A faint streak of light came from the sun in the west, while hordes of dark clouds seemed to chase it.

A faint voice escaped Reeta's throat, 'What happened, Mohon?'

'We're trapped in the middle of a hurricane,' Mohon Singh reported. 'I don't know if we've lost our way.'

'If we stray from our flight path, we'll end up in Venezuela. They'll welcome us,' Amoz Rangeela joked.

'They will not welcome us. We are children of coolies. So, not us. They will welcome the Amerindians, perhaps, their kindred. Venezuela has already claimed that western Guyana belongs to them. You would be welcomed, Amoz, but they won't trust the Indians and Africans.'

'Why? Why won't the Venezuelans trust us?' Reeta looked curious.

'Didn't you notice they've amassed all their armed forces at the border? They could march straight into Guyana any day. There's no reason for them to believe that we strayed due to a hurricane and mistakenly landed on the wrong land. They would see us as spies and treat us as such,' Mohon Singh explained.

Reeta was rather thrilled on hearing this. Let them apprehend her as a spy. She would then be a Mata Hari, willing to die for her country.

'It's quite unlikely they would throw us in jail.' Even amid the chaos of danger, Amoz stood undefeated as an optimist. 'They are luring all the Guyanese with money, settling them within Venezuelan soil; they might do the same with us too,' Amoz Rangeela remarked.

Mohon Singh remained silent, his gaze fixed ahead, a somber expression on his face. Soon, one dark cloud after another shrouded the front windows of the plane. Inside, the DC-3 throbbed and trembled, leaving Reeta feeling that the aircraft was quivering like a frightened pigeon nestled in the embrace of a colossal monster.

Reeta continued to ponder. Unexpectedly, the DC-3 descended abruptly, navigating through the darkness of the furious hurricane. Shortly after, the riverbank emerged from the gloom, and the DC-3 touched down.

Reeta shot a proud glance at Mohon Singh, but this time, no one came rushing to the side of the plane. It seemed that no one recognised the peril they had narrowly escaped, thanks to the brave pilot, Mohon Singh. Reeta simmered with anger in her thoughts. Mohon Singh's heroism was not to be ignored.

'Come down, Reeta,' Mohon Singh called out from below, raising both hands. Reeta suddenly slipped while descending the narrow steps of the plane. Mohon Singh sprang forward and caught her in a gentle embrace.

Reeta felt embarrassed and looked around in wonder. Did people notice the unsolicited embrace? She saw rows of shanties stretched out, with a handful of men diligently engrossed in their tasks.

'This is where we'll have our lunch; step over the slippery path carefully,' Mohon continued to hold her trembling hand.

Reeta walked carefully along the red gravel path, struggling in her high-heeled sandals. They reached a shanty house, where about fifty people were intensely occupied—their hands, legs, and faces stained with blood.

'Oh my gosh, an abattoir!' Reeta exclaimed in surprise. Slaughtered cows hung one by one.

A few Amerindians were skinning the carcasses with their long, sharp knives. Each person was splitting the carcasses into two parts with a large axe. The eyes of the dead cows stared eerily, shining brightly.

'Have you arrived, Mohon?' an Amerindian greeted him with a hearty laugh. 'Looks like you're a bit late this morning.'

'We got caught in a dark storm. I thought I would certainly sink into their whirling pit today.'

'The whirling hole accepts only pure sacrifices of the pure self. It would be happy to spit out a greedy trader like you back to your safety!' the old man laughed.

'Unlike us, you Amerindians are bound by a selfish brotherhood. We Indians are always plotting against each other, even though we settled here from our motherland, about 12,000 miles away. Of course, you'll consider us foreigners,' Mohon groaned.

The old man took no offence!

'Who have you brought with you? Never seen her before,' he asked with a friendly smile.

Mohon Singh introduced her. 'She is Reeta Majeed, currently a first-year student at Bishop's College in Georgetown.'

The old man bowed his head and nodded, grinning at her with his yellow teeth. Reeta extended her hand for a handshake.

'Ma'am, you might get blood on your hand if you touch mine,' the old man apologised. 'You're indeed welcome in our village.'

Reeta looked around, everyone else there seemed to be a rookie. Everyone grinned at her.

'Give us something to eat, Master. I am famished, but make lunch for both of us,' Mohon Singh pointed out.

'I know, I know,' the old man reassured. 'Now go and rest in your designated place. I'll take care of everything. It's all on my mind.'

'Come on, Reeta,' Mohon Singh invited.

They left the shanty on foot and strolled towards a small mound. Reeta was amazed as she looked down from the hilltop.

Far below them, the Potaro River meandered like an ethereal snake. The riverbanks were lined with rows of coconut and palm trees. In the far distance, three mountains stood together, their heads leaning against a wondrous sky adorned with red, yellow, and green hues.

Reeta crept closer to Mohon Singh. He took her hand, picked out her ring finger, and gently slipped a solitary ruby ring around it.

'Accept me, Reeta,' he whispered.

Reeta started trembling like a pigeon, unable to speak, her heart overflowing with joy, immersed in a blissful silence.

Since that Friday morning flight in September 1963, Reeta has accompanied Mohon on all his Friday flights, following the same routine. They would sit on the banks of the Potaro River, where she learned from Mohon the heroic tale of Chief Kai. Chief Kai canoed against the tide of the Potaro River to collect a giant pink water lily for his fiancée. With the flower in his hand, he couldn't swim back to her, and the ferocious tide carried him far away. He never returned, leaving his fiancée waiting and wailing behind the waters of Kaieteur Falls. Reeta trembled on listening to this tale in Mohon's resonating voice. She wondered whether Chief Kai would ever return to the waiting girl and silently prayed to Mata Laxmi for his safe return.

'One day, I'll also jump into the Mazaruni River to pick a 10-carat green diamond for you, Reeta,' Mohon said.

'And even you'll never return to us?' Reeta asked innocently.

'I'll gather a few stones of green diamond and sapphire from the banks of the Mazaruni River,' Mohon promised proudly. 'And, unlike Chief Kai, I shall return to you, Reeta!' he vowed.

Mohon Singh is vibrant and robust, a symbol of desire for all the girls in Georgetown. His charisma captivates both eyes and hearts, stirring wild emotions. Yet, why did Reeta's mind waver before the wedding? The hum of Siraj Sikdar's Vespa lingered, like the vibrant hue of the flame tree. Memories of quiet strolls past the college, sitting together in Newhaven Park, and reading under the deep blue jacaranda flowers exuded warmth.

'Maa, do I truly love Mohon?' Reeta confided in her mother.

Paromita looked amazed, 'You'll have to find that answer on your own.'

'I've asked myself repeatedly, but my heart isn't responding to the constant queries of my brain,' Reeta confessed. 'I've found no answer, Maa.'

'If an answer eludes you, perhaps it's best to rethink this marriage. It might be wiser to opt out,' her mother advised.

Paromita also wondered to herself. But was there any room for retreat? More than five hundred wedding invitations had been sent out. Word of the upcoming wedding, the wonder of Georgetown, was spreading through the neighbourhoods of Sturrock, Brickdam, Balham, Newhaven, and across the balconies of countless bungalows. All the eligible, unmarried students of Bishop's College—Nohana, Mohana, Trina, Kohana—were stung with jealousy. The paragon of beauty in Georgetown, Reeta Majeed, had transformed into an overnight social sensation.

In the weeks leading up to his daughter's wedding, Rehman often found himself at a loss. Why Mohon Singh? How did his hesitant feelings ferment within the family? How did the whispers of his pendulum-like mind reach his daughter as a command? And, how did the preparations for the long-awaited wedding of his beloved daughter speed up so quickly? How did it all happen so efficiently? It was as if Rehman Majeed had shaken a delicate pillar in Hades. With that first step, one after another, the values of life, faith, and instincts just slipped away on the winding stairs of uncertainty.

Was there intrigue in Reeta's wedding? Did the legacy of Indo-Guyanese cunningness weave a web of torment in Reeta's life? Did the centuries-old deprivation, lingering as a curse in the life of every Indo-Guyanese, cast its shadow over Reeta's fate? Despite countless inquiries, Reeta found no answers.

Nonetheless, Reeta dismissed all those negative thoughts and prepared herself to embrace her new fate. Dressed in an expensive *lehenga* and *kurta*, she sat silently on a sofa decorated with fresh flowers, her face covered with a golden Orhni.

'My name is Aliya,' said a little girl curiously peeking through Reeta's Orhni, and startling her.

'What is your name?' Aliya asked.

'Reeta,' the bride replied.

'My name means I am very close to Allah! What does your name mean?'

'I don't know, Aliya,' Reeta smiled at the question.

'But Abbu says every name has a meaning. Shall I ask Abbu?' the girl whispered, pointing at her father, the *Imam* of the mosque.

'Perhaps, it means the vapours of an empty shell,' murmured Reeta.

'You are like Tityra, a bird,' smiled Aliya. 'I must leave you now. Abbu is coming! *Dua* (prayer) will start. Bye! Bye!' Aliya ran back to her mother.

'You, Reeta Majeed, daughter of Paromita and Rehman Majeed, are prepared to accept the proposal of Mohon Singh, son of Bhagwan Singh, to marry you on the terms and conditions agreed upon by both your families?' the Imam Faizul Khan asked.

Reeta nodded silently, her face still covered by the golden Orhni.

Mohon Singh felt enchanted by Reeta's quiet posture.

'I must hear your voice, Kumari Reeta Majeed. Say "*Kabool*; I accept",' the Imam repeated his instructions.

'Labor omnia vincit,' the motto of Bishop's College, flashed into her mind. 'Whatever thy hand findeth to do, do it with thy might.' Reeta felt assured, thinking, 'Deeds conquer everything'. She silently committed herself to diligently fulfilling her duties at every turn of their impending married life.

'Kabool. I accept,' Reeta whispered audibly.

The eighteenth birthday ceremony that Reeta's parents had planned to celebrate with friends and family on 12 December 1963, had transformed, without her realisation, into her wedding day! But on that day, she neither understood the negative vibrations of her nervous heart nor recognised the heightened grandeur of the jealousies of her invited friends. The day simply rolled on, unawakened.

Chapter Two

The Blue-Eyed Bride

Paromita vividly recalls the November morning in 1943 when she waited with a pounding heart for the arrival of *Nil Ankhi Bodhuji*, the blue-eyed bride. The memory remains etched in her mind. How old was she then? On the brink of adolescence at the tender age of 15-16 and attending the tenth grade, Paromita already had a strong command over English. Her proficiency prompted her neighbour, Aunty Aji Bachaoni, Cheddi Jagan's mother, to seek her help that evening.

'The bride is expected to arrive next month. She speaks only English and doesn't understand Guyanese Hindi. Paromita, could you translate for her?' Aji Bachaoni appealed to her linguistic expertise.

With anticipation gleaming in her eyes, Paromita nodded emphatically, declaring, 'Aji, believe me, nothing is beyond the realm of possibility.'

Paromita's unwavering determination coincidentally

echoed that of Aja Jagan, Cheddi Jagan's father, the indomitable leader of Guyana. 'Nothing is impossible. If you ask with determination and keep an open mind, the possibilities are boundless. Our shared dreams can become a reality.' This mindset drove the Jagans to leave India in pursuit of a better life in Guyana, fleeing poverty, corruption, and societal burdens.

In 1917, on the final coolie ship from India, the Jagans embarked on their journey to Guyana, not knowing how profoundly this voyage would shape their lives. Their eldest son, Cheddi Jagan, the first of eleven children, would eventually bring Janet Jagan from America to be the bride of their household.

As the Jagans eagerly awaited the blue-eyed bride's arrival, the entire Indian community in Port Mourant shared the anticipation. Cheddi Jagan, a true son of the soil raised in Guyana, had attended Queen's College in Georgetown. After graduating as a top student, he left for the USA in 1937 to pursue higher education. After seven long years spent in pursuing a degree in Dental Science, Cheddi returned home in September 1943. Three months later, his American wife would be entering their home in Port Mourant.

The entire community of Port Mourant was preparing to welcome Nil Ankhi Bodhuji. Reflecting on these unexpected developments, Aji Bachaoni wondered if her son had strayed from her societal expectations.

'Where will the bride stay? Do we have enough provisions? I invested everything in our children's education, and prayed to Lord Shiva for Cheddi Jagan's success. What have we gained in return? Shouldn't we consider changing our home? Can the bride live in this humble abode?' voiced the concerned Aja Jagan.

'Why not?' countered Aji Bachaoni in a steady and resolute voice. 'I stayed here, didn't I? Cheddi Jagan grew up in this home. If my eleven children could thrive in this simple abode, why not the new bride?'

Aja Jagan tried to express his concerns. 'That's not what I mean. Janet is from a different culture. I heard they were once quite well-off. Adapting to our modest lifestyle might be difficult for her. She might even think of leaving with Cheddi, and starting a separate family.'

'There's no evidence that she'll have trouble adjusting with us,' Bachaoni responded calmly. 'She chose to marry a Hindu boy of her own will. I had my eye on several educated and religious Hindu girls for Cheddi,' she continued nonchalantly. 'The question of relocation by the firangi Bodhuji can be addressed later,' she grumbled.

'We were brought to Guyana as children from a completely different culture. Our parents struggled to cope with the unfriendly environment. What have we truly gained by migrating? We all had to accept this difficult situation and adapt to this way of life,' Aja Jagan agreed.

Despite his modest origins, Aja Jagan hailed from a

distinguished family. When Bachaoni's mother chose a husband for her daughter, she valued character over wealth. Despite wealthier suitors offering a substantial sum, she prioritised noble lineage. Bachaoni Jagan often wondered if her mother's migration to Guyana had truly elevated their social status. While India might have been financially modest, have they found the prosperity they sought in Guyana? Though their hopes were often shattered and their dreams trampled, Aja Jagan's determination remained unyielding. With an unwavering grip, Bachaoni clung to the family preserving its bloodline. Despite the hardships, both Jagan and Bachaoni took pride in upholding the family legacy.

'It would be in the bride's favour if she appreciates our sacrifices in raising Cheddi and our other children with our modest means. If not, it's inconsequential. Must I compromise my pride and tradition for the bride's sake?' Bachaoni responded.

Paromita reflects on those words of Aji Bachaoni uttered twenty years ago. At nineteen, she could not fully comprehend their wisdom. But now, two decades later, she understands their true meaning. Aji Bachaoni's words and aspirations had defined the limits of the Jagan family's ambitions. Paromita had always observed the resilience and love radiating from Bachaoni. If only, after marriage, Paromita could wield authority as adeptly as Aji. Perhaps she could have rescued her son Shovon from the clutches of the Madeiran woman, shielded Reeta from Mohon's disdain, and guided Rehman towards a more prosperous life. The thought weighed heavily on Paromita's mind: why couldn't she emulate Aji Bachaoni's solemn power, despite spending her entire youth in Aji's company?

Bachaoni experienced her first heartbreak after stepping into their new home in Port Mourant. Yet, she didn't waver. The company-provided residence stood amidst the sugarcane fields, rows of modest structures with mud foundations. The corrugated iron walls radiated intense heat during the day and turned frigid at night, beneath a roof made of banana leaves. A solitary wooden plank served as furniture. Despite her discomfort, Bachaoni remained determined. She vowed that the poverty they fled from in India would not engulf them in this promised land. Since both husband and wife had work contracts, their combined earnings amounted to a meager three shillings and four pence. However, uncertainties loomed during times of illness or work hiatus. Bachaoni navigated these financial challenges by turning canvas into clothes and layered blankets for her children. Wherever she found a patch of empty land, she planted fruits and vegetables—mango, guava, crab apple, and more. She saved every spare penny and raised her children with those hard-earned savings.

***

Bachaoni recalls that momentous day in 1923 at the sugar plantation. She had just dressed her eldest son, Cheddi, for school, a significant occasion for the family. Neighbours, both curious and astonished, gathered to witness the scene. Seeking approval, Bachaoni looked at her son. Aja Jagan had travelled to Georgetown to purchase the essentials, spending almost a month's salary. For the first time, Cheddi donned cotton clothes instead of the usual coarse ones, and Bachaoni took pride in her son, who now resembled a miniature gentleman.

'Wow, he looks like an Indian prince!' exclaimed several married women who had gathered from the neighbourhood at Bachaoni's invitation to witness the blessed occasion. Bachaoni's eyes sparkled with pride upon hearing their compliments.

'Oh, dear sisters, what good fortune that you could join us this morning! Now please offer your blessings to Cheddi. Today is his first day of school,' she called out excitedly to her neighbours.

'Why are you sending Cheddi to school so early in life?' inquired one of the neighbours in astonishment. 'You've been in Guyana for less than ten years.'

Bachaoni was taken aback. She sought an explanation for the connection between Cheddi's first day at school and their brief stay in Guyana.

'According to British law, we're not obliged to send children under ten to Sahib's school. You're sending your six-year-old son and wasting your hard-earned money on exorbitant tuition fees. Sahib's school teaches nothing but the values and history of their own culture,' the neighbour explained. 'Their textbooks talk about daffodils blooming in the snow in London. How does that relate to our life in Guyana?'

'All the students assemble every morning and pray to Lord Jesus. I've seen it myself!' the wife of the *Pujari* (Priest) from the Shiva temple asserted in a faint voice. 'They don't even recognise our Lord Shiva. You could keep Cheddi at home and teach him our own Indian culture and values,' she added, finally expressing her husband's religious concerns.

'My education is very limited, *Didi*. I want Cheddi Jagan to attend Sahib's school to learn their ways of life and understand how they achieve success,' Bachaoni replied humbly.

'What nonsense are you talking about? What do they even teach there?' rebuked another elderly woman. 'The black teachers at Sahib's school only focus on Christian teachings. They just want our Indian children to blindly imitate the white people.'

'Maseo, I believe that knowledge of the modern world cannot be gained without attending a proper school. In today's India, everyone is going to Sahib's school. My mother went to primary school. They no longer send children to a Tol or Madrasa,' Bachaoni objected.

'India is different. Here, the British government itself recognises the drawbacks of educating Indian children,' the senior lady remained resolute in her statement.

'What kind of evils could there be in Sahib's school, Aunty?' Bachaoni inquired with increasing concern.

'They claim that studying at a young age puts excessive pressure on the brain. It might even drive one crazy,' the neighbour stated with conviction.

'Then why do the British and the Blacks send their children to school at such a young age? The Blacks are ahead of us in public education,' Bachaoni pressed further.

Despite her questions, fear crept into her heart. Cheddi Jagan had just turned six, and the idea of him going crazy after attending Sahib's school was deeply unsettling.

'Their physical structure is different from ours. My husband has heard Sahib himself say that it's better not to send young Indian children to school but to put them to work in Creole groups. It strengthens their bodies and keeps their minds fresh,' commented the wife of the Imam, wearing a black hijab even in the company of women.

It was true. The British were not keen on educating Indian coolies. They had established Creole groups for the children in collaboration with the planters. Children under nine would join these groups, engaging in fieldwork, such as loosening soil, spreading manure, and planting seeds. At the end of the day, they would return home with 20¢, jumping joyfully. The planters framed this policy for the success of their plantations, arguing that this was not labour but a pastime, asserting that children participated voluntarily. They claimed the physical activity not only improved health but also enhanced performance.

'Not only that,' Fatima's mother added, 'see, my girl has already saved £10, a significant sum. I plan to buy her a saree when she grows up.'

'But why, Aunty? Fatima is already past ten years old; are you not planning to send her to school?' Madhuri inquired.

'God forbid she ever goes to a Sahib's school,' Fatima's mother exclaimed, placing a grieving hand on her forehead. 'May Allah protect us. My husband says we've been in Guyana for only nine years. After one more year, we'll secure our release from the plantation. Then, we'll move to the valley of the Essequibo River.'

'Why there?' asked Madhuri.

'It's our duty as parents to protect our daughter. When she turns ten, company representatives will come and forcibly enroll her in their school, where an African teacher will instruct her. My daughter might lose her modesty. Can we trust them? They're always ogling the girls, looking for ways to allure them.'

'Why not move to Georgetown instead? Why venture further into the land of evil spirits? Georgetown is only a hundred miles from Port Mourant, and there might be better earning opportunities,' Madhuri suggested.

'Even if we were to settle in Georgetown, the Sahibs would still cast their evil eyes upon her. But down there, the living environment seems better. My husband has already investigated it. I've heard that the place has promising earning opportunities and greater potential for investment. They've started harvesting paddy, acquiring rice fields at reasonable costs. We're considering to move. Let's wait and see what fate Almighty Allah has in store for us,' Fatima's mother replied.

'We're also coming along,' chimed in another elderly lady. 'Did rice ever thrive on this land? Some families from this plantation moved and ventured into rice farming. Since then, we've been privileged to savour the richness of rice. Otherwise, did the British ever provide us with this staple? Now, I've heard, the British want us to grow more rice. They'll pay us. If we cultivate rice, they can export it to India.'

History bears witness to this transformation. Rice farming started in Guyana in the 1890s. Early Indian settlers were deprived of rice as it was imported from India. The plantation workers relied primarily on bananas, fish, lentils, vegetables, and spices. Today, rice trading is Guyana's primary source of revenue.

Cheddi Jagan didn't enjoy his mother's conversation with the neighbours. He listened restlessly while tapping the toes of his newly purchased shoes on the ground to catch his mother's attention.

'Look, Maa, Aja is waiting. Shall we go?' he urged.

Bachaoni looked out and spotted Aja Jagan, now the driver of the plantation, waiting by the small pool on the other side of the range. He waved, beckoning his son. Bachaoni took a long look at Cheddi and then cast a questioning glance at the onlookers.

'Come on, my baby,' Bachaoni said, drawing Cheddi close and tenderly kissing him on his forehead. 'Return to me, my son, every evening with increased knowledge. Lord Shiva will guide you,' she silently prayed.

As his mother released him, Cheddi Jagan sprinted away. Bachaoni watched her son's retreating figure with a mix of pride and concern.

'That evening, I resolved, Paromita, that I too must escape the clutches of extreme poverty. Come what may,' Bachaoni later confided to a nervous Paromita after her wedding to Rehman, revealing how her vow to break free from the shackles of poverty had fortified her life journey.

To keep her word, Aji Bachaoni took concrete steps to improve her family's situation. She was committed to providing her children with the best education in Guyana, irrespective of the expenses. She leased farming land from the company to turn it into a source of family income.

She kept encouraging her husband to strive for more than just a life as a farm worker. 'You have education, wisdom, and intelligence. You've become a driver. You must aim to be an overseer. Show your sincere work ethic to the current overseer, and later, seek his support to be promoted,' she urged.

Aja Jagan expressed his concerns about the illegal activities associated with the jobs of drivers and overseers. 'I ought to stop those activities. But if I do, those miscreants will consider me an enemy, not an ally.'

Undeterred, Bachaoni dismissed her husband's reservations. 'If you hold your head high, no one can bring you down!' she countered.

Later in life, Bachaoni received similar warnings from her neighbours when she and Jagan decided to send Cheddi to Queen's College in Georgetown, about 100 miles away from Ankerville.

'You're making a huge mistake. You're going to lose your son; he won't return,' Zaineb's mother had warned.

'Why wouldn't I get him back, Aunty? With God's grace, I'm confident, Cheddi will return from boarding school at the end of each school year. During the long summer vacations, he'll spend time with his brothers and sisters at Port Mourant. He'll teach them cricket, the game of the Sahibs. His brother, Oddity, will play for the Port Mourant Cricket Team. He loves that game of the Sahibs. Please keep my boys in your prayers,' Bachaoni asserted.

'Our blessings can't compete with the influence of the Sahibs. They say that once our sons receive a British education, they don't return to their families. They become alienated. A gloomy day awaits you. You're sending your son, ignoring our advice. The consequences will soon be clear.'

***

Seated on the porch in Port Mourant, Bachaoni Jagan found herself reflecting on Zaineb's mother's words. Did she possess foresight that day? Could she have anticipated the negative impact a British education might have on Cheddi? Could she have known that he would marry a white girl from America and bring her into the Jagan household as his bride? Had Bachaoni compromised her own aspirations for this outcome? She had passionately fought with her husband to ensure each of their children attended the best schools available. Now, Cheddi Jagan was reaping the benefits of those efforts by bringing home a white bride. Would the younger siblings follow their elder brother's example? And why should the sisters be any different? They might tread the same path and introduce white or mixed-race husbands. Would a white bride have entered their home if a British education hadn't influenced their lives?

On the morning of *Bodhu Boron* day, before sunrise, Paromita noticed Aji Bachaoni sat alone on a mat in the long, narrow verandah, overlooking rows of large fruit trees she had planted when she moved to this home with Jagan 26 years ago, soon after their marriage. Cheddi was born here, as were Oddity and the rest of her eleven children. With each season and each puja, she would plant a fruit tree. Now, those trees had grown tall and were bearing more fruit than she and her family could consume. Her orchard was open to the community. Anyone could come and take as much fruit as they wanted from her orchard; there were no restrictions.

Aji Bachaoni looked pensive, her deep, piercing eyes fixed on the blue skies where ash-coloured clouds drifted. Paromita sat next to her in silence, afraid to break the stillness. Aji extended her right hand and embraced Paromita with deep affection.

Paromita looked up. Tears welled up in Bachaoni's eyes.

'Cheddi was our *Botto Brikha* (banyan tree). And continues to be. We had high hopes for him. He is our eldest son. His brothers and sisters loved and respected him even more than their own father. During our toughest times, Cheddi has always bound the family together with his counsel and advice. He is the pillar. We are proud of him, Paromita.'

'And you will remain proud of him eternally, Maseo,' Paromita comforted her. 'You shouldn't be in a pensive mood on this blessed day.'

'I'm just reminiscing about how all our dreams centred around Cheddi. I wanted a good education for him. I challenged him to prepare and qualify for admission to Queen's College. Aja Jagan was hesitant; the tuition fee for Queen's was incredibly high and beyond the means of a middle-income Indo-Guyanese family. But I was determined, Paromita. I promised myself that when Cheddi qualified for Queen's, he would find that his maa had secured the required finances,' Bachaoni beamed with happiness. 'My son met my expectations, Paromita.'

'I've heard that you worked very hard doing all sorts of odd jobs to provide for your children's higher education!'

'The credit doesn't go exclusively to me. It also goes to Aja Jagan. Even he surprised me with his commitment and love for Cheddi!' Maseo Bachaoni smiled.

'I'd love to hear more about that!' Paromita said eagerly. 'Would you like a drink, Maseo? Perhaps, I could make a cup of tea?'

'I'm observing an *upobash* (fast) for the welfare of Cheddi and his wife Janet,' Aji Bachaoni informed. 'Our *sanatani* faith requires that whenever we celebrate a blessed occasion, we should fast during the day to bring sanctity to the occasion.'

'I know, Maseo. My maa follows a similar ritual.'

'Cheddi graduated from Queen's College with high marks. He was ready for employment. But the job market was depressed due to the global depression from the Second World War. He wanted to become a primary school teacher. Cheddi admired Robert Burnham, his classmate Forbes Burnham's father. Cheddi saw in Robert how a head teacher could be a role model for an aspiring nation. Since Cheddi was qualified, he looked for teaching jobs, but the colonial rulers wouldn't let him join the primary school teachers' cadre. The requirement wasn't educational qualifications but faith—all primary school teachers had to be Christian. If Cheddi wanted to join, he had to convert to Christianity!

'Cheddi was demoralised. Aja Jagan was furious. But we all were in agony! We didn't know how to proceed. Weeks passed with grim faces shrouding our family.'

Bachaoni paused, and then continued, 'One late evening, Aja Jagan returned from work with a grin on his face. He was beaming with happiness. Waving a brown envelope under the hurricane lamp, he announced, "Here is the pass for Cheddi's further education. He will go to the USA this month!"'

'Had Cheddi secured a scholarship from an American university?' I asked.

'"Cheddi will secure a scholarship once he lands in the USA! This is just his passage money. I have withdrawn our entire life savings of $500," Aja said. I looked at him, his face glowing with happiness and pride. He declared, "Aji, the colonials may attempt to destroy our traditional Indian names, but I will not let them strip us of our God-given faith. Cheddi shall retain his faith!"'

'Janet, meet my mother.'

Cheddi escorted Janet by the hand and brought her before the waiting Bachaoni. Janet wore a purple saree, in a style that was new to her. A purple *bindi* adorned her forehead, and vermilion marked her hairline. Bachaoni looked up at her and couldn't help but admire Janet's beauty—her dark blue eyes as deep as the ocean, and the crimson vermilion in her golden hair, sparkling like a sunrise in the morning sky.

'Come near me, Bodhuji.' Bachaoni stepped forward to welcome the bride, extending both hands to feel Janet's beautifully henna-dyed hands.

'Bless me, *Mataji*.'

Janet didn't wait for the anticipated hug; instead, she knelt down, touched Bachaoni's feet, and picked up the dust, placing it on her forehead. A bewildered Bachaoni looked in awe.

It felt surreal. It was unheard of in Guyana—a white person bowing before an Indian woman. The mere thought of the gesture, let alone the act of touching the feet, seemed inconceivable. An astonished Bachaoni remained silent, the suspense of the moment hanging in the air.

'Will you not accept me as your daughter, Mataji?' Janet asked, lowering her gaze.

Paromita, standing beside Bachaoni, translated the bride's plea. Bachaoni snapped back to reality.

'Absolutely, my love, just wait for a few minutes while we perform the Bodhu Boron rites.'

The traditional Indian ceremony of welcoming a bride began with the *shonkho dhoni* (sound of a conch shell), followed by the collective ululation of young girls in sarees. Dressed in vibrant sarees and dresses, women of all ages recited prayers, turning Port Mourant into a dreamland. Janet, speechless, immersed herself in the sounds of cheers, laughter, and sacred chants.

At the end of the Bodhu Boron rites, Bachaoni warmly embraced Janet, guiding her into the house and seating her on a bed of flowers adorned with Indian lotus, blood flowers, lilies, Heart of Jesus, and sacred lotus.

Bachaoni studied the bride's face intently, 'Your face doesn't quite resemble that of a Sahib's, sweetheart.'

'So, how do I look then, Mataji?' Janet asked.

'The skin tone is quite fair, but otherwise, you look exactly like an Indian girl from the South.'

'Then accept me as an Indian girl. I wish to walk beside you, like an Indian bride, Mataji.'

That's impossible, Paromita thought. The bride must be lying, she's just pretending. Bachaoni, too, felt perplexed. Why was the bride deceiving even before joining the family? A foreign girl, a Bukra, living with Indians and adopting their ways? Impossible! Bachaoni had accepted the young foreign woman as her son's bride, but she couldn't shake the feeling that they wouldn't be living in this humble home in Port Mourant for long. Perhaps they were planning to relocate to Georgetown, and this stay was just a façade to avoid societal scrutiny. Why did Janet make this absurd request even before becoming a part of the family?

'We have many customs to adhere to, my dear,' Bachaoni cautioned, wary of Janet's alluring promises.

'I look forward to learning all those rites! Can I not master them with your guidance?' Janet asked eagerly.

'These traditions are stringent, requiring patience and time,' Bachaoni responded, still not entirely convinced by Janet's assurances. The Bukras had wielded influence over them for generations. And now, a Bukra's daughter was bowing in her house and touching her feet! Why? No white Guyanese woman would ever dare to do such a thing; it seemed unthinkable.

'I am your daughter, Mataji. I have promised to stay with your son until death parts us. I will stay with your family until I die. I am in no hurry.'

'Who else in the world would be happier if you could truly achieve that?' Bachaoni sounded hesitant. 'We can discuss these matters later. For now, please have a seat and enjoy some sweets.'

Paromita handed Janet a bronze glass, and the bride sipped the rose-flavoured syrup, quenching her thirst. Bachaoni presented a piece of round sweet from the adorned plate.

'Darling, savour the sweetness of *laddu* (an Indian sweet); it's a tradition,' Bachaoni encouraged.

Taking a half-bite of the sweet, Janet spoke again, 'I have one more thought, Mataji. I might falter at times and make mistakes in understanding the customs and rituals. But when I do, you will correct me, and, if necessary, even reprimand me.'

Bachaoni wanted to be moved by Janet's words, but found herself unable to fully trust them. Was this girl naive or overly confident? She didn't seem as sharp as a typical Bukra. Bachaoni wondered whether the bride might become an additional burden in her already challenging life. After all, Janet was American. Bachaoni had always hoped Cheddi would marry into a prosperous Indian family in Guyana. Many attractive Indian girls would have been glad to unite their destiny with the family of Driver Jagan. The family had borrowed significant sums to finance Cheddi Jagan's education, hoping that the investment would pay off. But then, he had brought home a foreign bride.

Bachaoni reluctantly accepted the reality. The bride might visit occasionally, then depart, free to go wherever she pleased, like the elusive dream of a dowry. But why, Bachaoni wondered, was Janet so eager to embrace an Indian identity the moment she set foot on the Guyanese soil? Why this fervent desire to shed her foreign persona? Could she end up causing even greater turmoil within the Jagan family by assuming the role of an Indian woman in an Indian household?

'Mataji, there's one more thing I'd like to share.'

Paromita looked surprised; tradition dictated that a new bride remain silent, yet this one was quite talkative.

Paromita, in turn, had to translate and relay everything to her mother-in-law.

'Go ahead, my dear,' nodded Bachaoni.

'I apologise for not bringing any dowry for you.'

'I did not expect any monetary gift from you, Janet,' Bachaoni responded firmly, feeling slightly offended. Discussions of solicited or unsolicited gifts between the two families were typically reserved for the men, and not discoursed openly with a new bride or bridegroom.

'Whether you expected it or not, we genuinely had no means to arrange a dowry,' Janet admitted gently. 'My father is quite poor. The cash gifts from friends and relatives during our wedding were already used to buy my ticket to Guyana. Only $1 remained.'

Janet is repeatedly using the word 'dowry', a tradition prevalent in India. Janet must have read lots of books on India before her marriage, wondered Paromita.

'Do you still have that dollar with you, dear?' Paromita eagerly inquired, having never seen an American dollar before. 'May I have a look?'

'No, I don't have it with me now,' Janet explained. 'I spent it on breakfast at the airport in Port of Spain. I was quite hungry, and now I have only 10¢ left. Would you like to see that?' she asked shyly.

Janet cheerfully unzipped her vanity bag and handed over the 10¢ to Paromita—a dime.

As Paromita was about to lead Janet to her room for

the night's rest at Ankerville, Aji Bachaoni made a request.

'I think it would be nice if Bodhuji pays her respects to Lord Shiva at the Shiva Temple. Paromita, will you please accompany her to the temple? It should be before sunrise. She could listen to our early *bhajan* (devotional song) sung by the assembled devotees.'

Paromita felt elated. The Shiva temple was only a few blocks away.

'You can explain our rites and traditions to her. It could be an adventure for both of you, strangers to this village,' smiled Aji. 'Besides, Cheddi might groan at the thought of going to the temple so early in the morning, even though he was always an early riser as a child. But seven years in the firangi land may have altered his routine.'

Aji Bachaoni then made her way towards the inner part of the home.

'I think Aja Jagan needs my help in entertaining our other guests.'

When they arrived at the temple, the *prarthona* (prayer) by the pujari had just ended. He was handing out yellow flowers to the devotees. Paromita picked one for Janet and one for herself.

'Hold this pure flower with both hands, say your prayers, and then offer it at the pedestal of Lord Shiva,' Paromita whispered to Janet.

'I haven't learned any Sanskrit prayers from Cheddi yet. There's no temple in Chicago,' Janet confessed. 'If there had been one, I would have visited.'

'My maa says that Lord Shiva responds only to prayers that come from the heart. We can pray in any language; it need not necessarily be Sanskrit shlokas. You may pray in English, provided it is genuine and comes from your heart. The language of the heart is what reaches the Lord,' Paromita advised.

Paromita held her flower and said her prayers. Janet watched her and followed the same rites. They both placed their flowers at the pedestal.

The assembled devotees watched in amazement. A white woman, clad in a red saree matching the red vermilion on her forehead, was bowing down to Lord Shiva with true devotion in her eyes, tears falling drop by drop onto the blessed pedestal—a sight unheard of in Guyana.

'*Jay Shiva debata ki jay* (Hail Lord Shiva), Hail to You!'

The devotees exclaimed together in admiration, three times in succession. Then, they paused momentarily before raising their voices again with a new tone.

'*Jay Nil Ankhi Bodhuji Ki Jay* (Hail the Blue-Eyed Bride). Let the blessings of Lord Shiva be bestowed upon her. Hail to our Blue-Eyed Bride!'

'What are they cheering for?' Janet asked.

'They are cheering for you, Bodhuji. They are collectively praying for you,' Paromita explained.

'The bhajan will start now. It's a traditional devotional song praising Lord Shiva.'

On the way back, they walked slowly, confiding in each other. 'It seems so surreal. Devoted citizens of a black country cheering for a white woman in their sacred temple, welcoming her into their midst,' Janet remarked.

'A son of our soil has married you, Janet. You are indeed a daughter of our soil. You belong to Guyana,' Paromita said softly. 'We Indians were transported to Guyana by the colonials. Our brothers from Africa were also brought here by the colonials for the plantation owners. The same happened to the Chinese, Portuguese, and many other nationalities, known and unknown, for over three hundred years. But, Mother Guyana has sheltered us and continues to nurture us. This is our land.' Paromita recalled the words of her history teacher at Bishop School and shared them joyfully with Janet.

'How do you distinguish, who is white and who is not? My father isn't fully white. He refused to meet Cheddi because he believed Cheddi was black; to him, all citizens of Guyana are black.'

'Who among your family attended the wedding?' Paromita inquired.

'It was a very small gathering of close acquaintances; even there, race and skin colour were issues! In the land of blessed America, where democracy prevails, and the rights of all human beings are honoured!' Janet flashed a peculiar smile.

'I knew racial discrimination existed in the USA,

particularly between whites and blacks,' Paromita admitted.

'But hidden discrimination also exists among the so-called whites. You know, my father changed his name to avoid discrimination in a southern white territory where he was employed. He's actually Jewish, but didn't want to reveal it. My grandfather was a devoted Jew. Jews were offered very few jobs in the USA, even though many started migrating there after the First World War.'

Paromita wondered what lesson she could learn from the Blue-Eyed Bride's confession.

'What an irony, Paromita. My grandfather feared discrimination in Europe, and my father feared discrimination in the USA because of his inherited faith. Yet, ironically, even he subjected his beloved daughter to discrimination because of her chosen boyfriend's skin colour! He threw his only daughter into the wild tidal forces of a strong river, leaving her to navigate a lonely journey of her own fate and destiny.' Janet wept, her body trembling with pain and agony.

As they approached Aji Bachaoni's home, Janet pointed out 'Your boyfriend is waiting for you, up there near the trunk of the big banyan tree!'

'He is not my boyfriend! We met only ten days ago at Ankerville during your Bodhu Boron ceremony. He also came from Georgetown, but we hadn't met before!' Paromita replied, a shy smile on her lips.

'He is a handsome boy! And he seems very interested

in you!' teased Janet with a laugh. 'If he proposes, would you marry him?'

'Marriage is a complicated process in Guyana. It's organised by the elders of both families. We girls have very little say in the matter, and it's the same for the boys,' Paromita confided. 'Besides, Rehman is a Muslim, and I am a Hindu Brahmin girl. Yes, Hindu and Muslim families do intermarry, but…' Paromita hesitated to elaborate further.

'You're stuttering with hesitation! Please, share your thoughts with me, Paromita,' Janet urged.

'It might be difficult for my family to accept a proposal from Rehman's family,' Paromita explained. 'We are an upper-caste Brahmin family. My grandmother didn't come here as an indentured worker. My grandfather had made a special trip to India to find an educated Hindu wife. They met at Mahatma Gandhi's Sabarmati Ashram. After finishing her schooling, my grandmother had applied for admission to a nursing college. Initially, she didn't want to leave India, but Bapuji asked her to go to Guyana and spread his message of non-violence. Gandhiji himself blessed their wedding,' Paromita clarified.

'We are an established trading family, but Rehman's father runs only a small grocery store,' Paromita mumbled.

'You're in love, Paromita. I know that feeling of uncertain certainty,' Janet said knowingly. 'I don't know much about Muslims. In my Jewish family, the term

'*Musalman*' was almost a taboo. Do Muslims celebrate festivals similar to Hindus?' Janet asked.

'I don't know much about Muslim customs in Guyana yet,' Paromita admitted. 'But my father told me that during his childhood, Muslims celebrated the annual *Tazia*. Hindu, Black, and even Amerindian families joined in the celebration.'

'What happens during Tazia?' Janet asked, her curiosity piqued.

'Tazia is held in memory of the two grandsons of the Prophet of Islam. About fourteen hundred years ago, the grandsons, Hasan and Hussain, were denied water during the Battle of Karbala in Arabia. My father told us that, back then, the entire village community would build a fake tomb, a *Tadjah*, using cardboard. They would decorate it with red and green crescents. The Tadjah would then be carried in a procession through the village streets. There would be singing, dancing, and mock stick fights to the rhythm of drums. Finally, some of the Muslim elders and youths would flog themselves as a sign of mourning. At sunset, they would float the Tadjah out to sea. My father was a regular drummer in the Tazia procession. Nowadays, Muslims don't observe Tazia in Georgetown. Instead, they celebrate *Mawlid*, the Prophet's birthday. They fast during the day, and after sunset, they host grand feasts, inviting all the neighbours. We've always looked forward to Mawlid since childhood. It's happening next month. Janet, you'll be able to join us! I'll let you know, and you can visit our home,' Paromita assured her.

***

Paromita still keeps that dime in a precious box. Despite its seemingly trivial value, the dime holds profound significance for her. It symbolises the experience, recognition, and the radiant convergence of embracing a new culture. Has Janet Jagan upheld these values throughout her life in Guyana, or have they gradually become a burden, not only for the Jagan family, but for the entire Guyanese Indian community and the nation as a whole? Paromita yearns for answers, but history is yet to respond.

Has Paromita's life unfolded within a whirlwind? She often finds herself in a corner, caught between two contrasting, yet equally compelling, women. At times, Aji Bachaoni guides her to one shore, while at other times, her elder sister Janet steers her in the opposite direction.

Skilfully guiding her through life's ebbs and flows, Janet taught Paromita the art of standing firm. 'Do not accept anything you do not wish to carry out. Resist it immediately. Polite acceptance leads to defeat,' Janet advised.

Bachaoni Jagan, on the other hand, stood for endurance, 'Paromita, speed up. Move forward with unwavering speed. What do you gain by standing still in the midst of a turbulent river? You face destruction, electricity, and fire—you burn yourself to ashes. Instead, move swiftly with the turbulent flow of the river's tides! Only then will you advance and make progress.'

Chapter Three

Seawall

'Oh Allah, I have never betrayed or cheated anyone, tricked a soul, squeezed an extra dollar, or given a dollar less. So why is there so much misery in my life?' Rehman Majeed grapples with this question, whether it's in the evening, morning, or while strolling down the Georgetown Seawall. He probes this question deeply within himself, rummaging through past memories, relentlessly searching for answers as the sun sets, exploring the remote corners of his mind. 'Is it a curse passed down from my ancestors? Or, have we made our lives bitter through our own deeds?'

Following Reeta's wedding, Rehman's daily introspection remains focused on his own heritage. He never questions or challenges the traditions, heritage, or faith of his wife, Paromita. She is an incredibly beautiful woman whose charm and astute advice could be credited with much of his success and happiness. He's been honest and hardworking all his life. Yet, his frustration isn't about himself; it's about those most precious to his heart—his son and his daughter. Why did Shovon's life take such a tumultuous turn? Why was Reeta's life disrupted by a hastily arranged wedding?

Rehman himself had to abandon his education to support their impoverished grocery-cum-convenience shop with limited delivery services. Yet, determined to break the vicious cycle, he ensured that his son received a quality education by enrolling him at the prestigious Queen's College.

The expenses of a quality secondary school education in Guyana, including private tutoring, were substantial. Despite their financial constraints, Paromita insisted that Rehman shouldn't give up on his dream of higher education, urging him to fulfil that dream through their eldest son, Shovon. And what has been the outcome of such sacrifice?

Shovon, now obsessed with a Madeiran girl, lives as a hippie. They live together without being married or engaged. And before they even turned twenty, they had a child. Should Rehman accept this child as his only grandchild? What future awaits this grandson, whom society views as illegitimate? Rehman finds it impossible to turn away when the child runs towards him with unsteady steps. He embraces the boy with a conflicted heart. After all, the child carries his blood. How could he reject this child's innocent love and recurring hugs? And yet, there are no plans for marriage, neither from his son nor the girlfriend.

Guided by his Islamic beliefs, Rehman disapproves of cohabitation. He counsels his son, emphasising the necessity of marriage in Islam. But Shovon disagrees, insisting it's not the modern way; no one wants to be bound by a man-made legal thread anymore.

Paromita explains that marriage is not just a legal or religious formality, but a recognition of their commitment. 'Being averse to it would bring shame to our family in Guyanese society,' she warns.

Shovon dismisses this traditional view as outdated. 'We don't see anything shameful in living together,' he retorts.

'Very well, but I don't understand, what's the allure of living together without marriage? Why? Marriage is a necessity. It ensures societal security and protection,' Paromita insists.

'You don't understand, Maa. Marriage is a binding contract. Even if we become incompatible, we'd be forced to stay together. We don't want to be shackled by this legal chain imposing enormous mental strain on our souls,' Shovon replies, visibly upset.

'You're wrong. Your father and I have been married for twenty-six years. Isn't our bond of love and respect visible?' Paromita counters.

'How many families like yours exist in Georgetown?' Shovon argues. 'Anywhere you inquire, you'll find cases of multiple marriages or three divorces between husbands and wives. Most marriages don't last more than four or five years. There's the endless ordeal of divorce proceedings and legal battles. We skip that by living together. As long as we desire, we remain bonded. Otherwise, we're free to part ways, without a fuss.'

'You only see the bonds; I do not,' Paromita replied, her tone turning bitter.

'Alright, then tell me, have you ever experienced the freedom you truly desire within your family life?' Shovon asked with keen curiosity.

'Why wouldn't I? Have I ever stopped celebrating our Kali Puja? My mother performed it, and I, too, will continue this tradition until I die. My daughter Reeta will carry on the tradition when she gets married. Your father has never prevented me from practicing our Sanatani celebrations.'

'You perform Kali Puja, even after converting to Islam. It goes against your adopted religion, Maa!' Shovon chuckled.

'What nonsense, son? You're born into a Muslim lineage; you're a Muslim yourself. I am a Muslim wife, but I have my own God. I have the right to invoke my God whenever I wish. Your father never prevented me! Rehman never asked me to wear the hijab, or to cover my hair and head! But both of his sisters who married in Suriname wear the hijab,' Paromita retorted, stung by her son's challenge.

The grouchy boy grew even more enraged by his mother's spiritual quandary.

'Is your God the same as my father's?' he demanded, but Paromita refrained from answering.

Rehman, having just returned home after a long day of work, was silently following the debate between mother and son. At this point, Rehman decided to intervene with his thoughts.

'Allah, God, and Lord are simply different names for the same essence, different ways of calling upon the same Power. Regardless of the name, it's a singular entity. Everyone is striving for the same purpose, seeking ultimate unity by following different paths.'

'Baba, I can't fathom your religious philosophy. I never could,' Shovon protested. 'Every society I've known or visited adheres to its own religious codes and rites. Christians venerate Jesus, Muslims worship Allah, and Hindus revere Shiva. In Guyana, we Indo-Guyanese are mixing together varied codes of different faiths to concoct a unique blend of worship for Allah, God, and Lord Shiva.'

'Baba has just returned home from a long day's work. Shovon, let's steer clear of this conversation for now. It's a delicate subject, and your father needs rest,' Paromita interjected wearily.

But hearing Shovon's words, Rehman began to groan softly.

'I didn't create chaos; I didn't negotiate with my Creator. I didn't blend religions. I simply embraced the inherent values of all religions. Because when the Day of Judgement arrives, and the final reckoning comes, we all will stand together before Allah. There won't be a separate judgement for Hindus. No distinct tribunal will be established for Christians. The Supreme Court will convene at a single venue, under one blue sky. On that day, souls will be divided based on goodness and sin, not on caste or religion,' Rehman spoke with fervour.

'Go tell the Islamic world about it. They might kindly slit your throat, just to avoid loving it,' Shovon replied with a sarcastic smile.

'Islam isn't just for Arabs; it's for all humanity. God created this universe for the benefit of everyone. He didn't impose discriminatory divisions among races and castes. But He did state that different communities should compete with each other to please Him. He is pleased only when we cultivate learning and acquire knowledge from the diverse aspects of His magnificent creation,' asserted Rehman. 'The mortal man should not hold a limited vision of One God.'

Rehman acknowledged the profound need of Guyanese society. History has shown that coexisting and retaining faith were imperative. When Indians arrived in Guyana, on 5 May 1838, 125 years ago, they were bound by indenture to start a new life. There was a compelling need to establish connections—religion, caste, and class judgements had little relevance. What mattered was the union of man and woman to build families. Delving too deeply into caste, class, and faith would mean dredging up their past lives, which they had grudgingly left behind in India, their so-called motherland. But why fixate on that history now? It only haunts and diminishes the power of the human soul.

'Was India so impoverished that it needed to send 2.5 million Indians into slavery, shipping them 14,000 miles away? Was India so pitiable that it continued sending thousands of slaves to colonial lords for eight decades? What a joke! A nation with a population of 40 crores couldn't sustain just 2.5 million skilled, but needy, workers? So greedy! So selfish! Generations chased the so-called wealth of distant lands, only to find shattered dreams. And when a few indentured workers returned to their motherland India after completing their contracts, they were not welcomed. No one in India helped them reintegrate into society. It seems that once our forefathers left their land, willingly or unwillingly, they couldn't return permanently,' Shovon pondered aloud.

'Baba, we bear the worst legacy of slavery. Our India's history is more disdained when compared to Africa's. Our ancestors willingly tied us into bondage without our consent, unlike the Africans who were coerced from Senegal, blindfolded and restrained by colonial slave traders. Our ancestors willingly thrust themselves into the shackles of servitude. Africa's ancestors did not. They fought back against the colonial raiders to protect the subjects of their burnt-out villages. The European historians did not recognise the immense economic and societal contributions of our forefathers as indentured labourers. Their struggles have been willfully stigmatised and unfairly tainted throughout each decade of our long journey,' Shovon reflected further.

The same story has been handed down through generations in every Guyanese household. There's no need to check facts. There is a peculiar mix of love and disdain towards India and Indians—a fascination with the culture, yet an odd aversion towards India and its government.

'Did India call us back after our indentured service ended, saying, "Return and reclaim your homes and lands; you've toiled abroad for too long"? Did the motherland call us back? No, they didn't. Even after India gained independence, did they understand our plight and ask us to return? So, why should we feel inclined towards Bharat or trust its culture? And why do we still carry the faith of India, the faith of Bengalis, in our lives? Even more, did independent India support our fight for freedom? Cheddi Jagan and Forbes Burnham pleaded with Prime Minister Jawaharlal Nehru for support, but both returned to Georgetown empty-handed,' Shovon asked Rehman sharply.

Shovon's words resonated deeply with Rehman. He was surprised that his son, his own progeny, seemed to understand their society even more profoundly than he did. Rehman looked at his son with admiration and love. Paromita stepped in, trying to close the conversation amidst this remarkable yet tense atmosphere.

But Shovon wasn't done yet. 'No, Baba, we won't get married. We prefer living together,' he declared firmly.

'I won't tolerate lawlessness. I've come a long way, supplementing my schooling by working as a night guard, holding onto my principles all the while. I won't let you ruin that honour,' Rehman's voice turned stern.

'Fine. You stick to your principles, and I'll stick to mine,' Shovon retorted, his anger surging.

Paromita rushed forward to mediate the escalating conflict between father and son.

'Even if you can't get along after marriage, you can file for divorce. Divorce is widely accepted in Guyana,' she soothed.

'That's the facade of society, hiding and covering up the truth,' Shovon remarked sarcastically.

'As long as you are my son, I won't allow you to indulge in living together,' Rehman asserted, unable to bear his son's defiance.

'I didn't ask to be born, Abba! Ask your Allah! I never asked to be your son. You brought me into this world without my consent. I never chose, willingly or unwillingly, to be born. So why should I now follow your wishes?' Shovon challenged.

Rehman pondered, 'Did any of us choose to be born on this earth by our own will?'

Could Paromita have fulfilled the expectations of her married life? Could she have heeded Janet's counsel to keep moving with the momentum? Paromita had rendered herself, as well as Rehman's entire family, astonished, moving like a fierce goddess from one corner to another to secure success and prosperity for her family. But has she truly succeeded?

Paromita had agreed to Shovon's decision to live with Rania in their large family home in Postel House. But, had this decision compromised her principles and her religious faith? Paromita wondered.

'I will not condone this sin. I will not be a part of this offence. If necessary, I will sacrifice my son. Instruct your son to go wherever he wishes with the Madeiran girl, but he must never reside in my house,' Rehman erupted with indignation.

Paromita objected, asserting that they couldn't impose choices on young people. Cohabitation had become a trend, and many kids of his age were following it. Shovon shouldn't be left behind. If he wants to live like this, let him do so for a while. Once the illusion fades, Shovon would return to his parental values.

'If there is desire, why not satisfy it elsewhere? Why do it in front of us?' Rehman remained steadfast.

'How could he live on his own, renting a flat?' The

thought tugged at Paromita's heart. Shovon wasn't even twenty-one yet, and he would have to leave his father's home? He had no income!

'Tell the Madeiran girl's father to settle it in shillings,' Rehman retorted, criticising the Madeirans, who, despite their origins, saw themselves as European, equal to the British. While the British may have committed wrongs, they didn't betray their own countrymen. In Rehman's eyes, the Madeirans consistently took advantage of Indians, Chinese, and Blacks. They elevated rice prices whenever possible, borrowed from the British to construct cheap houses, and then sold those houses to other races at exorbitant prices. To Rehman, they were unscrupulous and traitorous.

'Do you expect me to raise the daughter of an unscrupulous Madeiran? Absolutely not! I earn my income through means that are *halal* (legal),' Rehman declared.

'You're jumping ahead, aren't you? Let's take it easy,' Paromita whispered worriedly. 'Shovon isn't marrying the girl; he's just staying with her for a while. Why are you already thinking about marriage?'

'Are you supportive of Shovon? Do you endorse this sin?' Rehman stared at Paromita, bewildered.

'I do not endorse this sin, Rehman! But I will not distance myself from my son either. Otherwise, he'll leave my home. He'll rent a separate apartment. He's still very young, still my little boy. He just wants to stay with the girl for a while; why should I refuse and hurt his feelings? He will return to me when this illusion fades. If I drive him away now, he may never return to me,' Paromita implored, trying to sway Rehman.

Little did Paromita know, maternal sentiments were discreetly influencing her emotions. Had the illusion shattered over the past three years? Did Shovon return to Paromita? And did Paromita truly wish for such a revelation? Isn't Shovon bringing the same burden to Paromita's life that Janet Jagan once brought to the people of Guyana?

If multiple belief systems can peacefully coexist in Georgetown and Guyana, why can't two individuals live together without adhering to societal norms? Can't they coexist, with the bond of their minds as the primary foundation? Isn't that the reason they came together, caught in the tide of floating love? And if their minds veer in different directions, wouldn't they gladly welcome the change? Why disrupt a peaceful mind?

***

Paromita was in the kitchen, organising the family dinner she has planned for Shovon on the eve of his birthday. She has cooked his favourite dishes—Guyanese *khichuri* with generous portion of goats meat, chicken roast, and Paratha. While returning home in the afternoon, Shovon has brought warm patties from his favourite bakery for

Paromita. Rehman also returned home early and came down with Reeta. The whole family gathered at the table for a celebration, except Rania and Mohon. Taking his chair at the centre of the dinner table, Rehman looked for both absentees inquisitively. Both Shovon and Reeta understood his silent query.

'Rania has apologised for not joining us. She had a valid reason which I will tell you later,' Shovon politely explained.

'These days Mohon is getting frequent night assignments on short notice!' murmured Reeta.

'We will miss both of them. Let us begin our meals. Paromita has prepared many dishes for you, Shovon! Hopefully, Mohon and Rania will be able to join us later while we are still having our meals!' With a gracious smile, Rehman offers his thanks to Allah and starts serving the food to his children and wife. He looks solemn. They start eating.

Shovon breaks the silence!

'Baba! I took a long walk today through the streets of Georgetown. I spent the entire afternoon walking slowly and silently through my charted and uncharted neighbourhoods. I stopped and conversed with my friends, acquaintances and even strangers!'

'Why, Shovon? You have spent your entire life in Georgetown! You have visited every place while growing up.' Paromita asks.

'Maa! My head is clogged up with so many conflicting

themes and thoughts. I wished to unload those thoughts and clean my brain. The walk alone has done me wonders. I would share my mind with you all! Will you let me do so?'asks Shovon with excitement.

'We have always listened to you patiently, Shovon! And we shall always listen to you.' Rehman states, 'Free up your mind with your words.'

'Baba, we have debated among ourselves countless times, about our societal values, lifestyles, and practicing multifaith cultures. But Maa, we have never discoursed, surprisingly, on our current day political processes. And yet, this is crucial for our ongoing freedom movement and the need to get rid of the colonial British! Is it not strange, Baba?'

'Politics is a volatile topic. Let us not address that at the dinner table.' Paromita becomes tense.

'Why not, Mom?' asks Reeta. 'Shovon is correct. Talking about politics seems to be a taboo in this family.'

'You will deal with politics when you will finish the higher studies, enter the job market and gain experience. You both are still studying in college. You have to wait until your time to enter politics.' Rehman assures his beloved children, grabbing both of them with his both hands.

'Your Baba is correct!' affirms Paromita. 'Neither Cheddi, nor Forbes entered politics until getting firmly settled in their professional career.'

'I am not talking about entering politics, but

discussing among ourselves the current political situation. Political violence is affecting our everyday life. And yet it appears, the Guyanese youth are forbidden by an unwritten law of their elders that prevents them from questioning political moves or motives of their elders!' Shovon comments with a sarcastic smile.

'Shovon is correct, Maa. If we are not entitled to discourse on our political process, then why did both of you take us to various political rallies held in Georgetown? Until the age of twelve, we went to the rallies and marches with both of you. We saw uncle Burnham, we saw uncle Jagan, we saw Uncle D'Aguilar. He even kissed my hands like a European boy!' giggled Reeta. 'I was only ten years old.'

'Paromita encouraged me to leave my work on time so we could both take care of the kids during rowdy political rallies,' Rehman reminisces. 'Your Maa took the lead and, as usual, I followed her.'

'I wanted both of you to be aware of the various views and values of our diverse societies and learn firsthand from the process before turning teenagers,' Paromita defends herself.

'But what happened after we reached the age of twelve?' Reeta queries.

'You entered the middle schools. You were required to devote all your time to academic studies,' Paromita asserts.

'But why are you now forbidding us from

discussing the current political situation affecting our daily routine?' Shovon asks smilingly.

'Indeed, we are studying seriously. We have not neglected our studies before. We are not entering into the politics just yet!' Reeta quips.

Shovon adds, 'Don't be nervous, Maa. I would be very civil.'

Paromita shrugs and places the roasted chicken dish in the middle of the table.

'Reeta, would you please bring the *roti* from the oven?' Paromita requests.

Getting up from the table to bring roti, Reeta reiterates, 'I would be civil too!'

Everyone fills their respective plates. Rehman, as usual, silently thanks Allah for the food He has bestowed on the family.

'You may start your narrative, Shovon,' Rehman says smilingly.

Shovon clears his throat and starts talking. 'Baba! Maa! What is the date today? 20 February 1964. Tomorrow I will be twenty-one years old. Rania has gone to help her mom bake a birthday cake for me. She has expressed her heartfelt thanks to her mom for volunteering to bake a cake for her fiancé. Over the past twenty years in this home we have debated and argued countless times over myriad issues. But, we have never thanked either Baba or Maa because formal thanking within families is normally not practiced in our culture. But today, we would like to thank you for the amazing experiences you have given us to understand and appreciate our growing up phase. I still remember the day we visited Metropole Cinema in 1950. I was only six years old, and Reeta was only five. She wore a flowery frock with white stockings and black shoes. You wore a Saree, Baba was also formally dressed.'

'We sat about 25 rows from the stage, but we could clearly see the lighted staged adorned with fresh flowers,' Reeta elaborated excitedly. 'People were going up and down the stage, shaking hands with the guests and seated speakers, embracing each other, and singing songs in chorus. I loved all the ladies, wearing gowns with flowery hats and giggling together.'

'Yes, Reeta. It was 1 January 1950. All the people of Guyana had gathered at Metropole Cinema to celebrate the formation of Guyana's first political party, The Peoples Progressive Party (PPP). It was a multiracial party. People of all six races assembled at the cinema hall and, in one unanimous chorus, hailed the leaders of the PPP who would bring freedom to Guyana. They selected Forbes Burnham as Chairman, Cheddi Jagan as General Secretary, and Janet Jagan as Office Secretary. Other attendees included Moses Bhagwan, Peter D'Aguilar, Ashton Chase, Mooner khan, and Ranji Chandisingh among others. They were laughing, hugging each other, and assuring us in repeated speeches that freedom is not far away. Freedom is nearby. Our Freedom would shortly be snatched from the colonials. Back then, I did not completely understand what the word freedom actually meant. But, I understood it is a dream shared by everyone in our country. I am grateful to you, Maa, Baba, for this unique experience. How many Guyanese children of my age were that fortunate?!' Shovon trembles with emotions.

'I wished, Maa, that you were also on the stage, standing beside Aunty Janet, speaking to the people glittering on the stage,' said Reeta. 'It was a night of many Cinderellas, giggling, laughing and rejoicing. It is a musical dream coming true to an ogling child,' Reeta confesses.

'Yes, Reeta. Yes, Shovon! I also thought Paromita should be an integral part of the process. Janet is her confidante, Forbes is her neighbourhood elder brother. His younger siblings grew up playing together on the same playground. Cheddi already knew Paromita's family because their parents were mutual friends. Even their great grandparents were *jahajii bhai*,' reminisces Rehman, 'But, I never expressed my wishes to her.'

'That is the difference between your generation, Baba, and our generation. We share our resepctive dreams with our partners; but your generation did not,' gleams Shovon, finding a positive point favouring his generation.

'But Maa was a regular participant in the freedom marches and rallies. She never missed any rally organised by the PPP. Remember, Shovon, when Maa led us to the freedom rally? I held Maa's hand tightly; you proudly walked beside Dad. While marching, Janet Aunty bowed down and kissed me on my left cheek,' Reeta recalls.

It was 23 April 1953. The day is solidly etched in Paromita's memory. The PPP has earned a resounding victory, securing all eighteen seats across constituencies of the 1953 election. The PPP called out to everyone in Guyana—Coolies, Blacks, and Amerindians, for a unified freedom march. The Guyanese society obliged—thousands of people left their work in plantations, mills, factories and the Government offices to join the freedom march. Thousands of Guyanese assembled from all over the country, united by the objective of attaining Guyana's liberation from the oppressive rules of the British colonials. People of the six races stood united on the road to freedom. Up in the front, perhaps 500 feet away, Cheddi Jagan led the peaceful demonstration along with Forbes Burnham and D'Aguilar. Paromita marched shoulder to shoulder, step by step, with Janet Jagan and Jesse Burnham towards the Governor's house.

Paromita recalls Cheddi Jagan's historic words on that day:

> We find ourselves bound by invisible shackles—the British have ensnared our politics, nature constrains our every move. We are denied the freedom to advance towards the sea, and are unable to seek solace in the depths of the dense forest. Our minds, too, succumb

> to the grip of entrenched customs and practices. It is our solemn duty to break free from the chains that oppress and exploit us at every turn.

Burnham delivered a stirring speech. Stanislaus found inspiration in emotions, and tears of joy cascaded down Sidney King's face, mirroring the sentiment shared by Nikal Singh and all the other leaders among nations.

Finally, it was Janet Jagan's turn to be in the spotlight. The crowd erupted with joy, chanting her name—'Janet, Janet! You stand among us, the linchpin in our majestic victory.' Janet spoke:

> Six years ago, I welcomed a child into the world. Today, my life takes on a profound meaning as that child steps into adulthood. The journey of that child will continue; a challenging path lies ahead of him, and we shall be his guiding force.

The freedom march was orderly and peaceful. But, what is order and disorder? Paromita ponders silently. Aren't these words being merely the perspective of a turbulent mind? I am orderly when I choose to order myself, but when I am dictated, I certainly become disorderly.

'Allow me, Reeta, to revert to my thoughts and express them,' pleads Shovon. 'We got a rare opportunity to visit the past this evening. We may not get this night back again!'

Shovon's words bring Paromita back to the ongoing

conversations of the family at the dinner table.

'Fourteen long years have passed since that Metropole evening; Guyana has moved forward steadfastly under the collective leadership of the PPP. Many unfortunate events occurred within Guyana during this long period of struggle, but those did not break Guyana's resolve to snatch the freedom from British colonials.'

'Many of those events were divisive and were conspired by both external and internal forces,' commented Rehman.

'Baba, when we are united to achieve our freedom, is it not natural that the reactionary forces will create subversions and seed suspicions among us? It is in the colonials' interests to divide a unified nation and prolong their repressive rule.'

'But Forbes fell to the ploys of the colonials!' Rehman comments abruptly.

'It is a sweeping statement, Baba! I know you admire Uncle Cheddi. But, you ought not to be prejudiced against Uncle Forbes,' alerts Shovon.

Paromita gets anxious again. Will this conversation eventually lead to a flare up between the father and son? Shovon appears to be cool. And Reeta will manage her brother if the conversation gets heated.

'Allow me to sum up my observations on the PPP from 1950 to 1964. The PPP, remaining ethnically unified, steadfastly rallied for the freedom from 1950 to 1953. It won the 1953 general election. Cheddi Jagan was invited to form the new Cabinet. Cheddi created a government of six races by including Forbes Burnham, Janet Jagan, Sydney King and others in the Cabinet. But the first Cabinet was in a hurry. Jagan Cabinet adopted a confronting policy right from the beginning to antagonise the imperial powers. It refused to send a delegation to attend the coronation ceremony of Queen Elizabeth II. The Cabinet repealed a censorship law on "undesirable publications" enacted earlier by colonial administration. It encouraged workers of influential sugar companies to secure their rights by strike. Baba, looking back today as an informed graduate of Queen's college, I think these were all justified measures. But why was the first Cabinet in such a hurry to undertake these controversial measures within the first year of their ascension to power? Did the PPP leadership not realise that such measures will thwart, rather than speeding up, the Freedom Day?'

'Your point is correct, Shovon. I also wondered,' Reeta confesses and adds 'naturally, the colonial establishment at London would be worried that Jagan may bring about a possible communist revolution in Guyana. Everyone knew about the Prime Minister Winston Churchill's observation: "We ought surely to get American support in doing all we can to break the communist teeth in British Guiana". Undaunted, the PPP government passed a labour relations act on 8 October 1953. Alarmed by this defiance of the Jagan Cabinet, the British administration suspended the constitution of British Guiana next day, on 9 October 1953. Troops were deployed, for which Queen Elizabeth II had surprisingly already signed the order in London on 4 October 1953. The events of Black Friday provoked me to visit the Bishop's College library and dig into the past events. What I learned, Shovon, makes my heart tremble with fear and cry with sorrow.'

'Is it not a coincidence that we are both digging into the past societal events we grew up with? We have silently listened to these events at the dinner table when both Maa and Baba discussed the important events everyday. Back then we did not fully understand the significance or impact of those events on our future. But, the Black Friday of 1962 compelled me and many of my classmates at Queen's College to dig into the narratives of the then Guyanese media,' Shovon continues.

'The media reported that Jagan decided to visit London to protest his suspension. Burnham declared that he would accompany "his elder brother" to London. Both the leaders attended the debate in the House of Commons on 21 October 1953. But, the British legislators did not listen to their plea. Atlee said that his hands were tied. Defiant, Jagan, accompanied by Burnham, proceeded to our mother India, which had gained independence from the British just six years earlier. Both of them met the Prime Minister Jawaharlal Nehru on 20 November 1953. Yet independent India was unwilling to extend any support to its *Jaat bhai* (ethnic kin)!' Shovon remarks sarcastically.

'Nehru had Lord Mountbatten, the colonial, as its Viceroy! Perhaps he did not wish to confront the decisions made by the Jaat Bhai of Lord Mountbatten, the last British Viceroy. How could Nehru defy the cousins of his former colonial Governor General!' Reeta giggles repeatedly.

Rehman looks at his children with wonder. They had grown up. They look different. They are talking with a mature tone. They are not his little kids anymore.

'By crossing the *kaala pani* (the black waters), the Indo-Guyanese forefthers have wilfully surrendered their identity. They could not be treated as *desi jaat* anymore,' Shovon continues being sarcastic.

'You are wrong, Shovon. Burnham did not agree to go to India; Jagan went alone,' Rehman corrects Shovon.

'I assure you, Rehman, Forbes did visit India with Cheddi,' Paromita interjects.

'I have not seen that news printed in Guyanese press. I read newspapers diligently every morning!' Rehman asserts.

'You are forgetful, Rehman. The British forbade the Guyanese media from covering their visit to India. They censored all the news coming out of Delhi and London. Cheddi also met Indira, along with Forbes. Remember, Rehman, we got a letter from Sanchiatta, my politically activist cousin sister?!'

'Are you still in regular touch with her? We invited her to visit us at Georgetown a long time ago.'

'Yes, she promised to visit us when she's able to buy a tourist ticket herself. She wrote that Forbes is a handsome leader! She hopes to meet him when she visits Guyana and have a political chat with him. I promised her that I will arrange that meeting when she comes to Georgetown.'

'Colonials kept dividing us with false rumours to prolong their rule,' Reeta observes.

'Maa! Please do not divert me from expressing the thoughts clogging my packed brain. I must unload them and free myself from their heavy weight,' Shovon complains.

'Sorry, Shovon. Let this be your day!' Paromita concurs.

'Let this be our day, Maa!' Reeta interjects, slightly irritated at Maa's usual preference for Shovon.

'Following his return from India, Cheddi Jagan was kept under a house arrest together with Janet. The British Governor undertook repressive measures to thwart the freedom movement. Jagan was sentenced to six months in prison with hard labour for violating the restrictions on him for visitng the countryside constituencies. Moreover, many members of the PPP, belonging to all races, were routinely monitored, and their homes were raided in search of subversive literatures.

'During this repressive period, a few senior members of the PPP began introspecting on alternate political strategies to invigorate the freedom movement. Burnham came up with a few strategies. Similarly, Jagan formulated a few of his own policies. This was interpreted, perhaps wrongly, by the then civil society that came to believe, perhaps wrongly, that Burnham's policies would appeal better to the Afro-Guyanese, while Jagan's would ensure the allegiance of majority of the Indo-Guyanese. Both leaders decided to advocate their respective policies to their respective constituencies under the banner of the unified single Party, the PPP. The cynics of the civil society proclaimed that Jagan and Burnham have compromised their respective political ideologies for racial pragmatism. However, a few others believed otherwise. For instance, Sydney King, a leading Afro-Guyanese figure stayed with the Jaganite faction, while J B Lachmansingh, a prominent Indo-Guyanese leader, supported the political approaches of Burnham.'

Shovon stops momentarily and sips water from a glass handed over by Paromita. She was spellbound. She thought of her eldest son Shovon as a young Lecturer presenting a lecture to the students of Queen's college. Pride brought a calm smile on her face.

'The followers of both Jagan and Burnham contested the British Guiana General Elections of 1957 under the PPP flag. The Jaganites won 9 seats out of 15; Burnhamites won 3 seats, and 2 seats went to other smaller parties. But the election results show that the 1957 elections did not run entirely on the basis of ethnicity. The National Labour Front (NLF), founded by Lionel Luckhoo, an Indo-Guyanese, nominated Stephen Campbell, the first

Amerindian-Guyanese elected to the legislature. Moreover, one of the three elected members of Burnham faction of the PPP was, in fact, an Indo-Guyanese, Joinarine Singh. Similarly, out of the nine seats won by Jagan's PPP, one was secured by a Muslim, Sheikh Mohamed Safee. This means that perhaps ethnicity slowly crept into Guyanese society, long after the 1957 elections,' analyses Shovon.

'Jagan was appointed Minister of Trade and Industry. The British Governor, Ralph Grey, did not create the position of Chief Minister and retained the portfolios of Finance, Foreign Affairs and the Establishment. During his tenure, Jagan advocated for policies aimed at benefitting the rural Indo-Guyanese community, such as expanding land for rice cultivation and strengthening the power of unions within sugar industry to push for reforms.

'Burnham did not accept any position in the 1957 Cabinet. Instead, he founded the People's National Congress (PNC), a new political party aiming to advance the economic causes of the Afro-Guyanese. Forbes cultivated support from D'Aguilar to appeal to the Portuguese and Amerindians, expanding the PNC's electoral base. In 1959, Forbes contested the municipal elections and became the Mayor of Georgetown.'

'I have recently heard a joke on D'Aguilar. In fact, early in 1950s, Cheddi had urged D'Aguilar to join the PPP. He was reluctant. Cheddi humoured him, "Do you wish to change your family's life by selling fermented cereals and coloured water, or you wish to advance the life of multiracial, young generation of Guyana by joining the PPP?" D'Aguilar did not respond then. But, I am told, he regretted his decision later, and founded the United Force during 1960s to advance the cause of his people,' Reeta adds.

Shovon suggests, 'Let us now discuss the outcome of 1961 election, held to elect 35 members to a new Legislative Assembly. The PPP won 20 seats with about 43 per cent of the votes cast, followed by the PNC, which won 11 seats with 41 per cent of votes cast. The newly formed United Force secured 4 seats with about 16 per cent of the votes. Jagan was invited to form the government as the Premier on 5 September 1961.

'Burnham rejected the election results. The PNC vehemently protested Jagan's ascension to power, claiming that majority of Guyanese voters, 57 per cent, had indeed opposed the PPP. They organised mass demonstrations against the Jagan regime, calling for frequent general strikes and blockades against the elected government.'

Paromita admits, 'The period from 1961 to 1963 has been the most violent and divisive in Guyana's political history. On many occasions, the country came to a standstill, due to repeated racially-motivated violence initiated and carried out by both PNC and PPP. Spreading rumours, false apprehensions and mutual doubts were affecting the friendship among neighbours. Distrusts and doubts were reigning supreme among colleagues at workplaces. Friends conversed in public places in whispers! I confided to Rehman that Cheddi is treading a divisive path. Do you remember my words, Rehman?'

'Jagan decided to show his political power. His Cabinet imposed an austerity economic programme. Public taxes and import duties were raised, causing significantly higher impact on the Afro-Guyanese community,' Rehman concurs with Paromita.

'The budget actions contributed to the worst racial violence of Guyana. Massive fronts of rioters marched through the streets of Georgetown on 16 February 1962. The gushing rioters, filled with rage, attacked electric plants, water works, and parliament buildings. Even Jagan's official residence was not spared. More than 200 business establishments of Georgetown were either looted or put on fire. 39 innocent police constables were injured, while one police superintendent was killed. Jagan declared national emergency! The British administration deployed more than 2,000 troops and anchored two warships to stop the racial violence. This day is written in our history as Black Friday,' sobs Paromita in grief.

'It is rumoured among our students that CIA perhaps helped and funded the riots of Black Friday.'

'Furthermore, just last year, the Jagan government was brought to a standstill by an engineered labour union strike from April to July 1963,' Reeta gets excited joining the storytelling chain.

'To prevent the economy from sinking further due to the strike, Janet confided to me that Cuba would shortly ship oils to us!' Paromita states. 'But, Cuba's goodwill gestures were also misunderstood by us!'

'When a unified nation abruptly turns divisive, many rumours will naturally float. For instance, the Guyana United Muslim Party and Justice Party were allegedly created with CIA assistance to split the Indo-Guyanese voting bank. One day, the future will reveal the truth, Baba!' Reeta concludes.

'The PNC has argued that the current constituency-based electoral system unduly favours the Indo-Guyanese community, and has called for its replacement with a new system of proportional representation in the upcoming 1964 elections. Cheddi Jagan remains vehemently opposed to the PR system. What will happen over the next ten months, Baba? Will peace return, and sanity prevail among the political leadership of your generation before the election, Baba?' Shovon asks.

'I wonder what will happen to this country if riots and violence spreads further to other townships and to rural communities!' Rehman admits.

'I do foresee what shall happen to this country. The trend has already started within the suburbs of Georgetown. The Afro-Guyanese are moving out from the neighbourhoods where majority of inhabitants are

Indo-Guyanese. Similarly, Indo-Guyanese families are moving out from the Afro-Guyanese neighbourhoods. Both communities are conducting secret negotiations with interested families to exchange their respective properties. We trust each race for exchanging our land!'

'Even I have noticed a few of our Afro-Guyanese neighbours moving out, their homes now occupied by Indo-Guyanese families. Will this be a good trend, Shovon? Will it consolidate our society or disintegrate it further?' Paromita asks her lecturer son.

'I can happily vouch that if we encourage this racial trend, we will eventually follow the path dictated earlier by our Indian political grandfathers for India!' Shovon is determined that, this evening, his unique sense of sarcasm shall prevail on elder members of his family.

'Shovon, I do not understand what you are trying to convey to us?' Rehman projects irritatedly.

'We will follow the path of 1947!' Shovon declares triumphantly.

'Now, I am also puzzled, Shovon!' Reeta exclaims.

'After the midnight of 14 August 1947, millions of families in the Indian Subcontinent fled their homes and migrated to distant lands to retain their so-called religious identity. Fearful Muslims from East Punjab and West Bengal moved en masse to Pakistan. Similarly, fearful Hindus from Lahore and Dhaka migrated to India. We could tread the same path!'

'What do you mean, Shovon? Our Guyana would be separated?' Paromita enquires feebly.

'Yes, Maa! If we continue to dictate our future on the basis of ethnicity and remain insular within our *apni jaat* (ethnicity), the demand for creating separate homelands for each ethnic groups is bound to emerge! We need to reverse this trend of ethnicity aggressively, now or never!' Shovon asserts.

'Your generation, Maa, must realise that what is happening in your own society will forsake the future destinies of your progenies. You must take the lead to reverse this trend!'

'What if we fail to do so, Shovon?'

'In that case, we, the youth, will hold our own shackles and hammer, and march into the streets urging the elder generations, Baba, to revert your racial policies for keeping Guyana unified,' Shovon asserts.

'Our youth should not sacrifice their academic studies for harnessing political gains! You both are still studying as university students. We are paying tons of shillings as your tuition fees. You ought to complete your studies,' exclaims Rehman.

'Our new freedom march should be for retaining our own identity and existence in this land as a Guyanese. If your generation is unable to take up this cause, it is our obligation to carry out this struggle. Our struggle would be to shift our mindsets from ethnicity to a stronger unified freedom movement. This would be our priority.'

'Will the youth be able to carry out this struggle?' Paromita queries.

'If our student brothers in East Bengal could carry out this *sangram* (movement) back in 1952, why should we not be able to do the same in 1964?'

Shovon continues expressing his thoughts on Guyana's future.

'When Georgetown was burning on that Black Friday, on 16 February 1962, we, the elite students of the Queen's College, hid ourselves behind the closed doors of our classrooms, reclining our trembling heads under the study desk and jotting our wishes of teaming up with our cherished girls of the Bishop's College. Do you realise, Maa, how insular we had become from our surroundings? When I think of those days, I shiver in horror and feel ashamed of myself.'

'Even I could not escape from similar thoughts while waiting for Maa to come and pick me up from the campus of Bishop's College. I saw the rioters running on the streets, with flames in their hands and fury radiating from their angry faces,' Reeta recalls.

Paromita interjects, 'I had to run out to the Bishop's College. I knew, Shovon is a strong boy! He can handle himself; but my Reeta is a girl. She needs my protection!'

Reeta gets up from her chair and embraces her mother.

'That day, I realised, Maa, that I have a mom! She

would always be with me.'

'And that day, I realised that we, the youth of Guyana, henceforth, must not remain insular to the ongoing freedom movement run by our octogenarian leaders. We should raise our voices and affirm our rights for our own soil.'

'Your duty is to study diligently and prepare yourself for the future,' reaffirms Rehman. 'That's what Cheddi did. That's what Forbes did. They secured their professional career first, and joined the politics later.'

'I agree, Baba! But that route has become a dead end in the light of today's events. When values of our identity are challenged and the existence of our nation is threatened by the external forces, we, the youth of Guyana, must not hide behind the academic doors. We should follow our brothers of East Bengal, and march into the streets asking for our birthrights. We should not allow the colonials to conspire dirty ploys of ethnicity to generate violence and cultivate hatred within our unified society.'

'What situation now connects us to East Bengal?' Reeta queries.

'Tomorrow, 21 February, is my birthday! On that day, back in 1952, the students of the Dhaka University opened the black iron gate of the university that had been forcibly closed by the brutal police forces of Pakistani administration. They stepped into the dark "pitched" streets, and marched forward, shoulder to shoulder, hands bonded with each other. The first ten rows of boys were followed by rows of girls. Row by row, batch by batch, thousands of students marched to the parliament with a unified clarion call for acquiring Bangla as the state language of Pakistan. The language movement initially symbolised the rights of people of East Bengal to speak, study and run the administration in their mother tongue. The marching students faced brutal firings from the police! Blood flowed, drop by drop, on the dark streets. Five of the marchers faced the bullets; they dropped down on the streets, and later became martyrs. They sacrificed their precious life for the cause of their mother tongue. This sacrifice of 21 February 1952, the *Ekushey*, has turned into a universal symbol for advancement of culture and preservation of mother tongue of every race and ethnic group. The *Ekushey* shall remain immortal for the humanity,' Shovon relates.

'It is true, Shovon, on that momentous day, the students of East Bengal acquired for the entire humanity the right of every nation and ethnicity to nurture and speak their own mother tongue,' Reeta endorses with a qualifying note.

'We would emulate them from now on. Our unifying force is our Creole language. But, we have delegated Creole, our mother tongue, as the language of the poor and illiterates of Georgetown. We consider ourselves elites when we speak in English. Unless we love our own mother tongue, we would not be able to love our free nation. From now on, we, the youth of Guyana, will march on two fronts—first, we shall free ourselves from the colonials as a unified nation; second, we shall embrace Creole as a medium of expression of our culture and literature. We will resist any attempts for creating further racial divisions within the soil of Guyana, either by our own politicians, or by our friendly external forces,' declares Shovon.

'You look rebellious and defying, Shovon!' exclaims Paromita.

'Is that a recognition or a rebuke, Maa?' Shovon chuckles.

'You are resembling our future Pablo Neruda, a poet and a thinker,' giggles Reeta.

'Perhaps because the blood of Bengal runs through my veins. My ancestor, Lutful Majeed, boarded the ship from a port of Bengal. Is it not, Baba?'

Rehman nods in silence.

The doorbell rings. Shovon turns towards the entrance door. Someone is turning the keys from outside.

'I am sure Rania is back from her home. It's about the time. I have to be with her. Would you do the dishes, relieving Maa, please?' Shovon requests Reeta as he steps forward to the verandah.

'I will help Maa,' Reeta accedes.

'I will answer your query on another quiet evening, Maa,' shrugging his shoulders, Shovon steps into the verandah.

'Happy Birthday, Shovon. In just an hour, at midnight, your Birthday will begin!' Reeta exclaims.

'My birthday has already begun, Reeta! Does not the date on our Hijri calendar begin at the sunset? I have turned 21 after the sunset according to Islamic rites! I have already celebrated my birthday with my Muslim family.'

'Happy Birthday, Shovon!' Paromita embraces her son, 'Be happy.'

'Maa, according to Rania's calendar, I will be 21 within an hour. I will spend my birthday with my Christian fiancée, Rania, at midnight. This is the beauty of our Guyanese culture! We exist, we survive, and we advance, Maa!' Shovon reassures her worried mother.

Reeta repeatedly looks at the door longingly while doing the chores. These days, Mohon is returning home late, even past midnight.

***

Paromita could not sleep peacefully that night. Shovon's political narrative was vivid. She restlessly tossed within herself. Guyana's struggles for freedom in the 1950s commenced with the full force of the common Guyanese people. Every Guyanese marched forward under the collective leadership of their political leaders to jointly acquire the universal right of freedom in their motherland. No one cared about cast, creed, skin colour, faith or economic class. When was the invisible seed of division first sown among the PPP leadership? When did the silent whispers of a divisive politics for power and privileges begin to creep in, slithering like a snake in the dark, spreading clandestine messages of doubt and suspicion spreading from one mouth to another?

'Cheddi Jagan is a Leninist-Marxist. Janet Jagan is a Communist. She was a secret member of young communist league while studying in Chicago. Both Cheddi and Janet Jagan will seize assets of minority races and curtail their rights when they jointly assume power.'

The words spread like an octopus, reaching Bridgetown, Lethem, and Georgetown.

'Burnham will never allow the interests of his own people to be usurped by an untested socialist ideology.' Countering voices constantly hissed among the peddlers and pub-goers in the streets of Georgetown. 'Burnham draws the backing of the Americans. The US administration believes Forbes.'

'Let us not be a foolish race. Did you not notice US is still unable to control Cuba? Fidel ought to have a design for benefitting the Amerindians! That's why it is shipping oil to Jagan,' countering whispers spreads.

Rumours ripple even into the interiors of Guyana. Everyone is apprehensive, feeling threatened by the approaching dawn, when long-sought freedom will arrive, and perhaps repeat the midnight of India's independence.

Chapter Four

Blood Clot

Returning from college one day, Reeta found all her pots and pans littered at the foot of the stairs, with Mohon sitting on the doorsill. She grew concerned, wondering why Mohon was mad this time. Mohon's egoistic male way dictates that marital disputes should be broadcast for the whole world to know.

'You were not in the college at noon,' said Mohon Singh.

'How would you know?' Reeta replied with a question. 'I went to my friend's and watched a movie before returning.'

'Which friend? Tell me her name.'

'Cindry.'

'I came across Cindry at the campus; she was with Rumana. She didn't say you were with her,' Mohon retorted.

Unbeknownst to Mohon, Reeta kept her rendezvous at the park with Siraj a secret from her girlfriends.

'Don't remain silent. I spotted you in the green park! Siraj was with you.'

'Yes, we went for a walk and had coffee at the side café,' Reeta admitted.

'Why do you have to meet him?'

'What's the big deal? Everyone meets their college friends. If you get married, are you supposed to stop going out with others? No married girl can sit at home doing nothing, wondering in which distant land her lovely husband is flying!' states Reeta sarcastically.

'But you wouldn't go without my knowledge,' declared Mohon.

'And must I seek your kind permission early in the morning when *Kak* (cock) crows and you dress up for your flights along with your envious lady?' Reeta flirts with a sheepish smile.

Mohon remains angry, he holds his grudge for about an hour. Then he gets up, and gently collects the pots, pans and the pillows. He slowly goes up the spiral stairs.

'Come inside,' Mohon called Reeta, who was still waiting outside at the street.

Reeta slowly walked into their apartment, caught off-guard by Mohon Singh's unusually composed demeanour. Why didn't he burst out and throw away dishes, beds and mattresses out of the apartment, as he did many times before? Why didn't he raise a voice against her? Reeta wished he had, for that would have freed her from her guilt.

'Why did you have to confess it, Reeta? I would go through excruciating torture knowing this. My heart burns like hell when you meet your male college friends. If you must meet, never ever confess it to me! I am afraid our history of betrayal will repeat itself,' Mohon murmured softly, almost to himself. Reeta needed no further words. She realised that one day, she might step out into the uncertain world outside. She would reject the allured lust of a creeping snail. She yearns to be shackled and bound by an alpha male, oblivious to the envious eyes of an earthworm.

***

Paromita grew concerned when she noticed a black snake rising like a cobra's paw. There were whispers of doubt everywhere, and the peril was getting closer.

'I'm scared,' she confides in Rehman.

'Scared of what?' Rehman looks puzzled.

'Scared of freedom, scared of change. I feel like I'm once again about to be swept far, far away by the tidal waves of an impending catastrophe.'

'Are you scared of freedom, Paromita? Are you against the British being driven out?'

'I am scared of the impending 1964 elections; I am scared of Cheddi Jagan. He has run past three successive elections with the slogan of eradicating poverty, emancipation of women and spreading of free education for all the people of Guyana regardless of race, colour and creed. But, in the upcoming elections, Cheddi is campaigning vote for apni jaat. He seems to be spurting divisions in the name of freedom, sparking riots between Coolies and Blacks.'

'Cheddi needs to please his own people too; otherwise, the Indo-Guyanese votes will go to the United Front.'

'What are the costs of pleasing apni jaat? The past seven months have proven to be most violent in our history, with heinous violence engineered by the three political parties.'

'Paromita, there are many rumour-mongers among your circle. Don't listen to them. We have known Cheddi from 1943. You have welcomed Janet on the day of her arrival at Port Mourant. Maesee Bachaoni invited us! Have trust on Cheddi and Janet. They will never fail the aspirations of our six creeds.'

Rehman tried to brush off the matter. He had carefully followed Cheddi Jagan's political struggle over 14 years. He has unhesitatingly taken Janet Jagan on many road trips into the interior. He has silently attended the political discourses between leaders of the PPP, PNC and UF. He had listened to the profound thoughts of each Guyanese leader, be it Burnham, D'Aguilar or Cheddi. Each held a distinct and committed vision for a free and independent Guyana, though their chosen paths slightly differed from each other.

But, it wasn't only Paromita who was alarmed;

thousands of Indo-Guyanese felt the fright, as did millions of Afro-Guyanese. The British and American multinational corporations shared the same creep.

'Rehman, please try to understand my concerns. Look at the facts,' Paromita's requests turn stern.

'Just three weeks ago, on 6 July 1964, a passenger boat on a routine route was repeatedly bombed, immediately killing 38 innocent Afro-Guyanese workers returning home. Ironically, the same day, 5 Indo-Guyanese were killed within their own plantation. Before the anger of common Guyanese on the violent attacks could cede, on 17 July 1964, the PPP Headquarters was bombed, killing one person. Next week, GAWA, the trade union, called for a general strike among the sugar plantation workers. Which political group is inciting such cruel violence? Every evening, I wait alone in the drawing room scared, nervous and restless, praying for the safety of my family. Reeta, Mohon, Rania, Shovon and you—each of you are going out each morning on your own tracks, leaving me fearful and anxious for the entire day and night,'confides Paromita.

'Every morning, I wake up wondering, like many other mothers of Georgetown, whether our children will be a victim of the recurrent unpredictable violence during the day or they will return home, safe and unhurt. I worry for you, Rehman, until you return at night. If the violence continues at this rate, what will happen to our Guyana?'

'How are the kids tackling this situation, Paromita?' asks Rehman.

'They are quite silent, and perhaps resigned to the recurrent racial violence. I have noticed that both Shovon and Reeta go to their colleges together and often return home together.'

'Perhaps Shovon is protecting his sister.'

'Perhaps Reeta is counting on her elder brother's strength to shelter her. It ought to be mutual.'

***

'Oh Lord, why plague my body with such a predicament? Why not rather grant an early death?' Mohon Singh found himself lost in a sea of thoughts as he navigated the DC-3. No words were exchanged between them that evening. He had no desire to talk, not even to invite her to bed. He drifted off on the sofa, wrapped in a blanket, as if in an attempt to shield his entire world from the pain of the bygone days. Mohon Singh yearned to break free from a painful history.

'Demeanour of my master looks troubling. Could it be the lady at home triggering this?' Amoz Rangeela checked out the plane's door and entered the cockpit with a smile.

'Don't mess around with me, son of a pig,' Mohon Singh growled, 'Get out of here.'

'Master, why waste the anger meant for somebody else

upon me? Why not vent the anger where it's deserved?'

'How do you know I'm fuming over that woman?' Mohon Singh asked rudely, 'Did she call you?'

'Well, isn't that just quite obvious?'

Amoz Rangeela smiled a startlingly depressing smile. 'I've been with you for ten years, Master. You never battered me. You never scolded me with dirty words. Why this sudden shift within just six months of your marriage?'

Amoz Rangeela's remorse failed to resonate with Mohon Singh. A dark episode from the past was already clouding his mind, and he growled again, 'If my temper doesn't suit you, then leave my job.'

'Can I just leave you like that, Master? We're Amerindians. We respect our sense of loyalty. We're not the kind of people who flee every time they're faced with a slam or lured by a little extra cash.'

Amoz Rangeela's voice carried a combination of humility and pride.

Mohon Singh got even more offended upon hearing this. 'Don't invoke the virtues of a caste. Please, do not tell me the tale of pure blood. In truth, none of us is untainted; the blending of all kinds of blood between all castes has cast a foul odour across Guyana.'

'Perhaps, among your creed, Master. At least not in mine,' Amoz Rangeela gave a modest, yet proud, rebuttal.

'It is you people, along with the Blacks, the Chinese, the Indians, the British, and the Portuguese, who have traversed a thousand rivers and seas. We, the only original folks of Guyana, genetically belong to this land. Why would we bother to muddle our blood and not remain pure?'

It's true, and probably that is the reason why Mohon Singh felt so wounded. The African slaves traded from African homeland had managed to make it through as a slave during the colonial plantation life. Even after gaining the so-called freedom from the oppressive planters, they couldn't fully comply with a free life. Indians, on the other hand, willingly abandoned their own freedom behind a colonial Bharat, opting for a life of servitude in the hope of a livelihood, money, and a secure future. The Amerindians staunchly resisted both Dutch subjugation and British dominance, rejecting the French-imposed servitude. Instead, they forged alliances with the British, Dutch, and French, proudly retrieving the escaped African slaves.

The Amerindian boasts, 'Our girls never forfeit their dignity; neither do the boys snatch it away.'

Mohon Singh interjects contemplatively. But, did Indian women truly retain such a deep sense of personal honour? Instead of surrendering their bodies to the invaders, did they not willingly leap into the flames, the pyres they themselves had lit? The bold steps of Indian women for retaining their honour have been written in textbooks and passed down orally for centuries. But then, who among the Indo-Guyanese dared to break free from the fetters of the dignified past? Who has left behind a resentful legacy for Mohon to carry shamefully into future generations?

Mohon repeatedly questions his own lineage and deeply probes into his ancestral roots. Though he found no evidence, Mohon had long concluded, since his teenage years in Georgetown, that the blood of an unknown Black man flowed through his veins. He comes to the dereliction that his future would be shadowed by the betrayal of a shameless Indian women.

In an effort to diffuse the tension, Amoz Rangeela offers, 'Master, don't misinterpret my words. I've brought you fresh coffee; my mother brewed it this morning. Shall I serve one cup for you? Perhaps, it'll help ease the rage.'

Mohon Singh, takes a moment to contemplate, reflects on his foolish anger vented towards Amoz Rangeela. He's been with me for more than ten years and never botched any of my jobs. What benefit would I get by unloading the anguish of my abhorrent past upon him?—he thinks.

Mohon gives in to his inner thoughts and says, 'Okay, bring me my cup. Let me savour it.'

Amoz cheerfully fetched him the mug of coffee, noting, 'Mom had prepared it herself for us. Can you detect the flavour?'

The DC-3 plunged forward in a violent thrust, the engine sputtering, just as Mohon extends his hand to hold the mug.

Mohon curses, 'Damnit, would she not spare me even

a second of peace in my life. She is as jealous as Reeta.'

Amoz comes in to help, asking, 'Shall I hold it for you, master?'

Mohon, in his utter frustration, retorts, 'Are you nuts? You'll nose dive this bastard straight into the rainforest.'

Mohon, unable to comprehend Amoz's intentions, thought he was attempting to control the plane.

'We'll be blown away in no time. I'll handle it right away. You better hold on to the mug,' he announces.

Amoz Rangeela reassures him, 'That's what I wanted to hold, not your angry engine.'

Amoz holds the cup while Mohon Singh remarks that the DC-3 seems unusually loaded today, with the engine making a loud, troubling noise.

Amoz chuckles, suggesting that the plane might be having a rough day, much like Mohon. He points out that the plane is fully loaded, which could potentially lead to operational strain.

'Money will be good today,' remarks Mohon.

'Then only you will benefit, Master,' Amoz responds. 'All I care about is my pay. I'm just your paid sidekick.'

With an open laughter Mohon promises, 'I will give; I will share.'

He then talks about closing a business deal with a new client and making Amoz a partner in the trio. Amoz assures that he would serve Mohon as a trusted, dependable partner for life.

'Now, get me that coffee,' Mohon chuckles, 'Otherwise the deal will again hang in the sky just like ourselves.'

As Mohon savours his coffee, he is lost in the past once again, pondering if his animosity towards Reeta is genuine. He questions whether Reeta is willingly treading a reckless path in the dance of happiness, akin to the capricious woman who spilled the mysterious laws of nature into his blood.

Mohon recalls the day when he was around eleven or twelve, a sudden awakening enveloped him, and he ran off to his octogenarian grandmother questioning her outright how the *Kailla* (black) blood got onto him. Fearing that he might say something reckless, the Granny swiftly presses her palm on his lips and silences him with a *shhh*.

But Mohon is adamant, demanding to know it. He bares his body to flaunt his physical features, features that a typical Black man possesses—frizzy hair, upside-down lips, and a solid black torso. He confronts his grandmother, asking if he was adopted or collected.

'Absolutely not, Mohon,' the grandmother reassures him. 'You are my grandson, the only one among us! After six girls, finally, a boy. Never speak those dirty words again.'

'Grandma, Dadi! Why am I seen as a Kailla? I've studied science and biology. Tell me, how did blood of a Black man come to stream through my veins?'

Grandma, not truly blinded, had anticipated this moment since Mohon's birth. She, along with

Mohon's mother, had lived with this fear, waiting in trepidation for the day when scary questions would surface. The day had come.

'Tell me, Dadi, who was that proud beautiful woman? What adulterous act stained my body because of her joyous coiled moves?'

Mohon caught her gaze with a question lingering in his life ever since. No answer was provided, though, only a reminder of a bygone tale.

Convulsing in a panic, Grandmother exclaimed, 'No, no, that is not a demonstration of an art, but the pinnacle of a cruelty, a cruelty ingrained in Guyana.'

Unyielding, Mohon refuses to budge. Sporting a sardonic smile, he queries, 'Did the cruelty of the entire land descend solely upon us, grandmother? Was the burden rested on my shoulders alone to bear?'

Gingerly, Grandma responds, 'Everyone has suffered. Everyone had to endure torture in Guyana. But perhaps, the share of tyranny we got was more than others.'

'Why? Were our greed more willing and so prioritised ahead of others?'

'No, Mohon, because God wronged us.'

'That's a convenient answer, Grandma. Blaming God to absolve yourselves of guilt?'

'No, God is responsible. Solely responsible. There was no remedy in human hands. Never had been,' Grandma grumbled, almost as if making a confession.

'Why is that? Due to poverty? You were abandoned by your parents? You endured fathomless wants and deprivation?' Mohon's sarcasm hits Grandma deeply.

'God is responsible for making us beautiful. Open your eyes and see, Mohon. We are beautiful. Indian women are beautiful. Not the Chinese, not the Portuguese, not the Blacks, but us. That beauty brought us disaster. We were forced to bow down to the demands of chauvinistic male.'

***

It all began in 1907.

Grandma retraces her steps down the memory lane, recalling a history fraught with hatred.

'The name of this land is Guyana, also called the land of a thousand rivers. But Mohon, in my perspective, Guyana is a land of a thousand tears, a land of pain, a land contaminated by corruption.'

'I seek justice, Sahib.' Budho Singh stood defiantly at the door of George Beauford, the British gentleman and owner of the sugar plantation. George, engrossed in experimenting with his friend's newly acquired rifle, was enveloped by the bellowing gun smoke. The smell of gunpowder lingered in the air. Right then, Budho Singh showed up at Sahib's garden.

Edward Jenkins, a ship captain by profession who had just brought the rifle from London, was boasting of its superior range. The bullet could traverse the sugarcane fields and almost reach the borderline of the distant green forest. George Beauford, skeptical of his friend's claims, declared, 'I want to check it myself.'

He aimed the rifle straight across the sugarcane field at the cluster of slaves gathered around the heap of sugarcane at the edge of the jungle. George Beauford, with a sinister cackle, remarked, 'If you're right, my friend, the tallest among the slaves is going to be no more today. Lately, he's become a bit audacious, bugging for more shillings and not sparing a single girl in the range.'

'Do I understand that he dared to interfere with your share of girls?' noted Edward Jenkins.

'Of course not. I never dig a girl who has ever been rubbed by a slave,' George said proudly as he stared through the crosshairs of his rifle, aiming at the target.

'How can you ascertain? Where are the girls on your plantation? How many girls are there in the entire country? They're not everywhere, but in places where they exist, everyone is desperately vying to claim them.'

'I can assure you that my women have never been touched by other men,' George Beauford asserted himself firmly, pressing his index finger on the trigger. Seconds later, the tall black image in the distance dropped to the ground.

Born as a free man, surviving as a slave, and dying as a loyal driver of plantation workers, the man's life was even worse than that of a free slave. A menacing smile appeared on Sahib's lips—cruel, exposed, and repugnant. 'Abraham was an asset to me, a skilled driver, and a competent supervisor for the coolies. Now, I must find a new driver.'

The *driver*, not of cars or of buses, but of slaves, of labourers. The term was coined by plantation owners, and it has been the most coveted position on Guyanese plantations for over a century and a half. It comes with honour and power, adorned with ample opportunities to abuse them. If you seek a prince in the plantation hierarchy, look no further than the driver. The driver's role involves complete control and power over the coolies. Leading them in groups to the sugarcane fields, distributing their tasks, and ensuring they work according to their abilities are all part of the driver's responsibilities. He also checks for any attempts at evading assigned works or secret conspiracies to escape from the plantation during the deep dark nights through the deep forests of the plantations. Upon returning to the range, the aura of power remains undiminished. The driver oversees their accommodation, food, and even resolves disputes among the coolies in the range. In essence, the plantation owner is the omnipotent Sahib, and directly below him is the driver, the majestic overseer. However, in the world of coolies and labourers, the driver reigns as the absolute shadow master. This is why the position of driver is highly tempting. Whether Madeirans, Blacks, or Indians, everyone aspires to become a driver. The fortunate one who secures the position transforms into a prince, commanding the respect of all the women on the plantation.

Edward Jenkins, the captain of the slave ship, has spoken the truth. His greatest challenge in the shipping business was the scarcity of women. Despite the abolition of slavery in 1807, the indentured labourers were essentially treated as slaves. Women were especially scarce and difficult to obtain, and, if found, their price was exorbitant. This shortage of women deeply impacted slaves, labourers, and traders.

Among the West African slaves, girls constituted about one-fourth of the total, increasing only to one-third by the nineteenth century due to rampant raids of slave traders into the deep interior villages of African west coast. However, the demand always far exceeded the supply. Ships transported slaves from port to port in eastern coast of the US, with able-bodied young girls fetching higher prices long before reaching the shores of Guyana. African women, prized for their strength and ability to work, brought unbridled happiness to owners, slaves, and drivers, contributing to the expansion of the slave population.

Picking up a young girl on a plantation meant both financial gain and physical satisfaction. However, the quest for girls proved futile as they were continuously sold to white owners across West Africa. Guyana, not easily accessible, had its own unique dynamics. The Portuguese, primarily from Madeira, zealously guarded the few girls they brought into their community. The white planters usually averted forceful acquisition of Madeiran women. But this courtesy was not extended by the Dutch or British, who disregarded the hurt feelings of the other castes residing within the plantation.

The Chinese, hesitant to completely trust the British, not only refrained from bringing their own women but also contemplated returning to their artisan lifestyle upon the expiration of their contracts. However, desire frequently led them to explore sparsely secured camps for illicit connections, culminating in the emergence of the mixed-race community, now identified as Chainadouglas.

Though Indian girls started out scarce when the indentured labour trade commenced, by the early 1900s their numbers had gradually increased reaching almost equal proportions with their men in Guyanese society.

'I want justice, my Sahib George. Award me my lawful rights, Sahib.'

Budho Singh pleaded in front of the coffee table, bowing his head in respect to Edward and the plantation owner, George Beauford.

With raised eyebrows, George Beauford glanced in annoyance, gun smoke still curling out of the rifle barrel and a lingering scent of cordite wafting through the air. Shifting the barrel to his left hand, Beauford frowned and asked, 'Who allowed you to enter my private quarters?'

'Pardon me, sir,' Budho Singh explained. 'Zabaniya was holding the iron gate. I didn't listen to him and sneaked in through the fences seeking a just trial from you. I know, my Lord, that you are great. You will give me justice.'

A faint smile crossed George Beauford's face at the compliments, but he ratcheted up his irritation. 'I am currently on holiday, spending time with a friend. Your forced appearance, escaping the eyes of the watchmen, has been rather impolite, and I must say, I could persecute you for this.'

Witnessing George's crimson eyes, Budho Singh prostrated himself at Beauford's booted feet, hands pressed together. 'Due to my hot temper, I unexpectedly lost my civic duty, sir; please forgive me.'

Edward Jenkins lit his pipe which was packed with freshly roasted tobacco brought from Jamaica, its intoxicating smell filling the air. Offering guidance to his friend, he said, 'The poor fellow may have momentarily breached discipline in a fit of anger; you are free to flog him at your discretion. But shouldn't you be aware of the specifics of complaint before passing judgement?'

'I quite know it all. The Indian breed is terribly emotional,' George smiled at his friend. 'Either a Black driver sneaked into his house at night, or some other Indian driver attempted to seduce his beautiful wife. Listening to these routine complaints made my ears prick up. I will never purchase Indian coolies again; they can't labour like a Black man. One Black man can make up for three Indian coolies. They can't abide by discipline, and diseases continue throughout the year.'

Jenkins looked a little surprised.

'I used to think the fertility rate was very low among Indian coolies. They suffered from malaria and dysentery, and have now grown disease-resistant. Why come here and die?'

George laughed and tapped on Budho Singh's skull with the tip of his left boot.

'Look at him! A slave brought by your colleague from Calcutta.'

This mindset mirrors the perspective prevalent among plantation owners who take the indentured labourers as slaves despite the abolition of slavery. Those dwelling on the plantations were, anyway, nothing more than just slaves.

'When I brought this labourer five years ago, he weighed about 130 lb. How much does he weigh, now? Hardly 101 lb, they won't eat anything. All they do is, save money and lose weight.'

Budho Singh was stupefied to hear Sahib's words. He is not a slave. He is an indentured labourer. He considers whether to remind this to Sahib or not. However, he suppressed his urge for now.

Sahib continues. 'Alongside the range, the Indians will grow all kinds of vegetables and eat potatoes, but never touch eggs or meat; they are all-out vegetarians. It is forbidden in their religion. The truth is, it costs money to get them. Why spend it?'

George Beauford grabbed the rifle lying by his side and pointed the barrel at Budho Singh's chin, shoving him a little.

'Stand up. Look at him. He never bought a dress. He is still wearing the same clothes he had on when he left India. Tell me, why they will not be diseased. They are inviting death themselves.'

Edward Jenkins is tuned in to his friend's tendency to shift from one topic to another. In an attempt to satiate his curious mind, he steps forward and begins questioning Budho Singh.

'What is it that you're seeking justice from us now?'

'The driver broke into my quarters, ransacked my things, smashed the trunk, threw away the pots and utensils, and even confiscated my salary,' Budho Singh bursts into a hundred of complaints against the driver.

George Beauford, with a wry smile and crooked eyes, glances at his friend.

'As I've told you before, this complaint is a common occurrence in every Indian household on the range, on every plantation.'

Edward, looking for further clarification, asks, 'Did you commit anything wrong? Did you break the discipline of the range?'

'I am innocent, Master. The driver says I skipped work, which is untrue. I can outwork every Indian on the plantation.'

'Then what made the driver upset with you?'

Budho Singh bows his head, a faint line of embarrassment cloaking his dark face. With his eyes lowered and toenails nibbling on the green grass under his feet, he acknowledges, 'The driver has ill intentions towards my wife, my lord.'

'Found anything new other than I told you?' George Beauford glances at his friend.

'You, return to your work in the plantation right now. I will conduct your trial during the weekend,' Beauford instructs.

Edward Jenkins found himself intrigued by the incident. His entire life had been spent on ships ferrying black slaves. When the British abolished slavery, the ships got engaged in transporting indentured coolies from India to various destinations like Mauritius, Trinidad, Barbados, Cuba, and Guyana. Occasionally, he has to spend a few days with some plantation owners as a guest or friend; he rarely witnesses plantation life up close or the life of the coolies. There is another matter to consider. Though explcitly acknowledged as coming from a Caucasian background, deep within his heart, he concealed that his lineage is not exclusively of pure Caucasian descent. While his appearance may not reveal it, his roots do. A British vicar from the seventeenth century, on a mission to evangelise the natives of West Africa to Christianity, ended up marrying an African woman. Jenkins, the result of that union, carries the weight of acknowledging his mixed heritage in his veins.

'Justice must be swift; delaying does not add to the owner's authority,' Jenkins reminds his friend. 'I am eagerly looking forward to witnessing how it is administered at the plantations.'

'Well, if you want to experience our justice system, then,' George Beauford laughs, 'Of course, let's proceed. Judgement will be rendered this afternoon after the workers return from their day.'

Jenkins stands up, and George hands him the rifle. 'Hold it.'

Jenkins feels a shiver of terror running down his spine. He reflects George Beauford testing the rifle's range just a while ago. The Black driver still lies on the ground, possibly already dead.

'What will happen to him?' Edward points in that direction. A sly smile appears on George's lips. 'They won't dare trace the dead back to me. I am the owner here. Let us deliver justice to Budho Singh.'

George rises and exits the bungalow. The two friends begin walking along the sugarcane aisle, with Budho Singh following. By that time, his initial anger had transformed into doubt, and he was pondering whether coming out seeking justice was a good idea or not.

Kanak Kumari was squatting in the yard, trembling with fear and apprehension, flanked by a few Indian girls who were frantically cursing her. She couldn't stop

Budho Singh from seeking justice, they doubted that Sahib would ever deliver justice; rather, Budho Singh might face punition.

Kanak Kumari only gazed at them with her helpless eyes and muttered, 'He has such a bad temper! He left before I could explain or even realise what was happening.'

In the light of these circumstances, Kanak Kumari is not entirely at fault. She had been married for less than six months, having tied the knot within three months of her arrival in Guyana. Budho Singh had transferred 1,500 shillings to Kanak Kumari's old man, a significant sum worth three years of sustenance for the Brahmin family, along with silver ornaments.

Her Brahmin father fell for the trap one day when a British representative visited his home in South India and inquired about his worship practices. He offered him the job of a temple priest in Guyana, and agreed to bear the entire costs of his travel along with his three unmarried daughters and wife. He assured the Brahmin Pujari that thousands of Indian citizens are awaiting a qualified priest to preserve their faith in a distant land and to pass on their faith among their progenies. In the imperial colony of Guyana, Brahmins were almost nonexistent, and so were the Imams. Worship was a distant echo. But, providing opportunities of worship within the plantations proved wonderful for quelling frequent trepidation and quieting turbulences among the slaves. Faith leaders were in great demand in the plantations. Hence, planters enabled regular congregations at simply-built temples and mosques.

Kanak Kumari's father answered the call of faith, embarking on a British ship with his three daughters, in pursuit of spiritual duty and purity. However, the idyllic plan was shattered when the Guyanese planter disregarded faith and religion, and instantly consigned him and his daughters to the sugarcane fields, a hundred miles from George Beauford's estate.

Budho Singh, on finding about the old man's three unmarried daughters, donned his finest attire on the day of his leave and approached the Priest at the plantation temple. There, he sought Kanak Kumari's hand, offering shillings in abundance. The nuptials took place, with Budho Singh adorning his bride with a silver nose ring that he had once brought from a Georgetown bazaar, marking the beginning of their new life in January 1906.

Kanak Kumari didn't ask for much upon her arrival in this new world; her aspirations were modest refuge and respite. She sought solace from the clutches of intense, lustful gazes that had ravaged her body during the three-months-long ship journey she and her sisters undertook. Yes, the Captain allocated their family a separate enclave due to their sacred Brahmin class. The Priest dutifully and devotedly offered prayers attended by the indentured labourers daily at the dock. In the face of fear, she endured the advances of lascivious eyes. With divine assistance, she safely landed in Guyana—a testament, perhaps, to the spiritual fortitude of her Brahmin heritage.

In the aftermath of her wedding, over the last six months, Kanak Kumari has found happiness. Budho Singh enveloped her with love and protection, and shielded her from the toils of labour. Even when the driver pressed for more work, Budho Singh took it upon himself, defending Kanak Kumari.

Yet, could Budho Singh escape the looming disaster? Did the untamed waves not carry the ominous clouds of doom to their shores? Kanak Kumari trembled. Since her arrival at the plantation, the driver, Nakfal, had fixated his eyes on her. Despite his persistent eyeing, Nakfal refrained from pouncing at once. Well-versed in the plantation ways, he bided his time, betting the opportunity would present itself.

In their modest abode at the range, with a bed constructed with two planks on two-inch bricks, Kanak Kumari initiated her family into a humble setup where community cooked meals were served during the day, and nights found rest on the ground. Budho Singh, upon his arrival on the plantation, had procured two brass bowls, three round plates (one of bronze), and a blanket, which he later sold at a good price. Presently, a stained canvas bag serves as a quilt against the cold or as a shield from marauding mosquitoes. These simple possessions filled Kanak Kumari with immense pride, her admiration further fuelled by Budho Singh's financial astuteness as he proudly recounted his exploits to his wife.

'No one could ever deceive me. I was cautious when I crafted the employment contract. The overseer suggested receiving the salary in Indian rupees. I categorically refused. Shillings were the agreed-upon currency. I insisted on receiving shillings.'

'Money is money,' Kanak Kumari commented with an uninterested gaze. 'Just take it. Why fight with the boss over nothing?'

'You lack farsightedness, my dear wife. You see, one Indian rupee is valued at 18¢ here. Why settle for less? The overseer presumed he could outsmart me, deeming himself a gentleman and me a barbarian. Little does he know, I've passed my sixth-class exams back home. Why should I listen to him? He insisted that Indian rupees and Guyanese shillings are of equal worth, and I would be paid in rupees. I disagreed. I pulled out the employment contract and pointed out the clauses before his eyes.'

Budho Singh was adorned in a shirt with a dhoti wrapped around his waist. 'Right here, it's mentioned that the owner will pay the labourer in shillings. I stand by what's inked on paper. The British never falter in honouring their written words.'

'Is that how you managed to amass so many shillings? You know, there have been many couples married over long periods, some for a decade, others for fifteen years, and even more. Surprisingly, they claim to have no savings.'

'How in the world could they?' Budho Singh interjects.

'They are naive. Once they agree to be paid in rupees, there's no turning back. The British have laid out the rules—men receive one shilling a day, girls get 50¢, and children receive 20¢. But instead of shillings, they are all paid in rupees. They ought to return to India to get those funds.'

Indeed, only a few workers, following Budho Singh, have successfully secured wages in shillings. Most Indian labourers simply fail to comprehend this multinational web of currencies and end up losing in the plantation gamble. Budho Singh stands out as an exception, a thorn in the eye for many. Add to that, there's the allure of Kanak Kumari.

Budho Singh has other hallmarks, as well. He had pledged not to let Kanak Kumari join the Creole band for work. 'Why not?' Nakfal inquires. 'The range rule stipulates that everyone on the plantation must work. All residents in the sugar company's household, including wives and children, are obliged to work, provided they are more than seven years old. Is your wife also below seven?' Nakfal chuckles.

Hearing this, the Indian coolies hanging around erupted into laughter—old and young men, women, and children. On plantations, there are few separate kitchens; most are common kitchens, serving everyone in society. Cooking becomes a community affair, fostering conversations, igniting debates, brewing rumours, and passing on sinister whispers. Budho Singh found himself ensnared by Nakfal in the midst of it all, right in front of Kanak Kumari, who was squatting on the ground, rolling out dough to fry into rotis. Kanak Kumari blushed with embarrassment.

Budho Singh affirms, 'There is no agreement for Kanak Kumari's job. She did not sign the employment contract upon her arrival. She will not work in our plantation. She has no employment contract with the British Government.'

'How come she boarded the ship without a contract? Did she arrive on a sky-chariot?' Nakfal laughs.

'The work contract was made with my father-in-law. There is no clause stating that his daughters must work too. Kanak Kumari is not bound to work.'

It's a fact. Brahmins are brought in to perform religious rituals, worship, and serve the temple, as stated in the employment contract. It wasn't possible to include a clause mandating their families, including their sons and daughters, to work.

Nakfal, however, refuses to concede defeat. He contends that the agreement was with the British government, not with the plantation owner.

'If you wish to stay on the owner's land, you must work. If you don't want to employ your wife, then build her a house outside the owner's land, not here.'

Nakfal delivered his direct orders. As a driver, he has

risen above other African drivers, catching the eye of George Beauford. He cannot compromise his masters' interests.

'If that's what it must be, I will stay well beyond the boundary wall,' Budho Singh firmly retorts, 'Kanak Kumari will not set foot in the sugarcane field.'

The elders placate Nakfal saying, 'Don't argue with Budho unnecessarily. Nakfal, just wait a few more days. Budho might be a hard nut to crack, but when the time comes, Kanak Kumari will herself join others. All the girls eventually do. Why should she be an exception?'

Age begets experience, and wisdom takes root.

Kanak Kumari fails to figure out why Budho Singh vehemently opposes her working with the Creole band. All the girls, adorned with blood-red amaryllis, gleefully join Nakfal to work in the sugarcane fields. As the girls depart early in the morning, the range becomes desolate, leaving Kanak Kumari feeling terribly lonely. Her anger towards Budho Singh flares up occasionally because she thinks his obstinacy is the root of the continuing unrest in the entire village.

In less than a month, once again Nakfal attempts to lead her to work. Budho Singh offers a compromise—he will pay Nakfal a premium of 20¢ as long as Kanak Kumari is refrained from joining the Creole band. Kanak Kumari became incensed when she learned about this.

'Why won't you let me join the Creole band? All the other girls do.'

'That's strenuous work, dear. Cutting, cleaning, and clearing the jungle isn't easy. It's hard labour.'

'But everyone manages it. Why can't I?'

'They've grown up on plantations, tackling treacherous nature from childhood. You're a Brahmin's daughter; you haven't learned.'

'I will learn. I have arms and legs, and strength. I'm not disabled. What's preventing me from working?'

'No, under no circumstances. Nakfal is eating into my hard-earned money, but I won't allow you to go.'

Budho Singh has a number of good reasons to prevent her from going to work. Having spent six years on the plantation, he has witnessed and experienced much injustice. He is determined to shield Kanak Kumari from lawlessness, especially the perilous trek to the sugarcane fields. Along the route, numerous ditches and sinkholes must be navigated, drains crossed, and canals swum through. The absence of bridges, coupled with the chest-high water levels, makes the journey challenging, particularly for girls.

Besides the obvious dangers, Budho Singh seeks to further protect Kanak Kumari from other threats, such as the piranhas, and predatory crocodiles lurking in the water—along with Caimans, stingrays, and the venomous Bushmaster snakes. Electric eels pose the risk of an electric shock. The Creole group faces these dangers daily, and there's no guarantee of escaping them unscathed. Budho

Singh, well-acquainted with these perils, wonders how he could subject Kanak Kumari to such inevitable dangers, considering her ignorance. Despite Nakfal's persistence and cunning, Budho Singh is resolute that Kanak Kumari will not join the Creole trekkers, regardless of the cost.

Nakfal, just as sly, seizes the opportunity one afternoon when Budho Singh is away. Despite the ban set by Budho Singh, Nakfal commands Kanak Kumari to join the team, claiming George Sahib's command overrules that of Budho Singh. Faced with a dilemma, Kanak Kumari is worried, as Budho Singh's two-day absence has already stretched to four. The fear of danger looms, and Nakfal intends to slowly tighten his grip on her.

The driver, adept at exploiting his power, grabs the chance to assault Kanak Kumari during the master roll calls, held thrice a day. The ritual, especially the morning roll call, subjects labourers to sheer discomfort, standing bare-bodied in lines while enduring mosquito bites. Nakfal sees this as a perfect chance to bring Kanak Kumari under his control, and other girls rally to support him.

'Come on, sweetheart, check out what we can accomplish. How long will you confine your love for your husband? If we can do it, why can't you?'

Kanak Kumari acquiesces. She recognises that the hindrance is not from her but from her husband. Now, when he is absent and cannot enforce his prohibition, why object? Gleefully, she joins the Creole team, adorned with flowers, eager to savour this new experience.

It took nearly two weeks for Budho Singh to finally return home, his heart yearning. There was no escape. The master ran roll calls thrice a day—morning, evening, and midnight. Moreover, the road is too long, spanning a distance of ten croshes (an old Indian unit of distance, roughly 2 miles or 3.2 kilometers each). While he could have attempted to meet Kanak Kumari in hiding during the night, it was not feasible for him to return to his station before morning. Fourteen days later, upon discharge, he rushes back home, only to find Kanak Kumari missing. Impatiently lying on the plank, he waits as the evening descends. Where is she? He abruptly wakes up from nap when he hears singing voices of village girls outside. In a jovial atmosphere, Kanak Kumari strolled homeward across the vast expanse, flanked by the Creole band, with Nakfal beside her. A surge of blood rushed to Budho Singh's head as Nakfal was caught in the act.

'Bloody traitor! You have defrauded me by taking my money.'

Nakfal laughs out loud, like the devil.

'If the wife concurs, why are you angry? I have followed Sahib's rules,' Nakfal laughs, casting a strange glance at Kanak Kumari.

'Don't you ever take her out again,' Budho Singh threatens. 'You have betrayed me.'

'Kanak has grown into a woman, Budho. Such a robust

physique, oh, the contours of her thighs, like a budding gourd. If she prefers to go with us, who are you to object?'

Hearing Nakfal's comments, the accompanying girls fall into unashamed giggles.

Unable to stand Nakfal's sarcasm, Budho Singh lowers his head to charge like an angry bull. Fortunately, the elders managed to restrain him. Nakfal is not just an ordinary Indian; he is the envoy of the plantation owner, the driver, and the untouchable. If that doesn't go into his head, then Budho Singh is simply a nut.

However, Nakfal's honour has been scathed. As the driver, he should never be trifled with. How dare Budho Singh ever try to strike him? As a retaliation for his outrage, he storms into Budho Singh's den, ransacks everything, and throws them outside into the yard.

'Bukra is a Sahib,' Budho Singh contemplates, a little confused now about involving a Bukra in this affair. 'Is this the right thing to do?'

'I will ask for my justice from the Shahib. I will show him the documents,' Budho defiantly states. 'He will punish Nakfal, the betrayer.'

'Don't go to a Bukra. He will not give you justice,' Budho Singh was cautioned by the elders. 'And then again, judgement for what? Why shouldn't the wife go to work? All our wives are working. Why shouldn't yours?'

Budho Singh refrains from providing explanations. Discussing the topic of honour would implicate almost all the girls in the community. What's the point? Budho Singh retains courtesy and reiterates the old argument, saying, 'Her father did not contract her for work. Why should she work then?'

'You're going to a Bukra; will he heed your complaints? Impossible! Can't you see, they are the ones squeezing our lives dry like the sugarcane and ditching our bodies into the swamps, the marshlands, and along the edges of the Atlantic?'

'What difference would it make to you if I filed a complaint?' Budho Singh retorts. 'You're opting to hold onto your job. When did your contract expire—ten or fifteen years ago? Come on, redeem yourself now. Follow the brave examples of the Black man. They leave the plantation as soon as their contract expires!'

'Nope, we're not complaining. We simply accept our fate and the fact that we have opted for residing in this country. This is our country.'

'What is fate?' Budho Singh protests. 'Black men were slaves; the British set them free. We replaced them. We were free men who willingly became their slaves.'

'Not a slave, Budho Singh. We are indentured labourers,' the aged Lakshya protests vehemently, trying to control himself.

'Yeah, labourers only in name. Nonetheless, a life worse than that of a slave—wasn't it better to be redeemed? Wasn't it better to leave the plantation? Plantation is not our country. The entire Guyana is our homeland.'

'Where would we go with redemption? The sugar company gave us a place to stay, provided us with food, and allowed us to grow produce on their land,' Lakshya Singh explains. 'With the ocean in front and floodwater behind, we are trapped in the middle. Where do we go from here? How do we escape?'

'Move over to Georgetown and start a business. Why are you still sitting around on an expired contract?'

Lakshya Singh grins, 'Many of them had already been acquitted. What happened to them when they moved to Georgetown? Most of them died from hunger on the streets. No food, no clothes. Some went lunatic; no one offered them shelter. No one dared to call. Labourers freed from plantations are untouchables. People are afraid to touch them.'

'All bogus. Only the Indians are cowards; their minds are small. The Chinese never panicked. They joined hands together to build prosperous businesses! They left the plantation as soon as their work contract ended. Black men also leave when the contract is over. They move from one plantation to another, greedy for more money. The Madeirans leave, too. It's only you who won't go; you're afraid to try something new. If the Black slaves had not left the sugar plantation en masse, the British would not have brought Indians to fill the labour gap. We were substitutes of Blacks. We have subjugated ourselves deeper than blacks. The Madeirans are a distinct race; they are Portuguese carrying European traditions. The British pay them more and harbour no animosity towards them. Rather, the Madeirans were welcomed, given job opportunities and business permits, and provided bank loans. So why persistently cling to this soil? Year after year? Generation after generation? You came on contract; leave now!' Budho Singh advises.

'Where to go? Who will take us back? India doesn't want us,' Lakshya Singh smiles a deep, sorrowful smile. 'Returning at our own expense requires a substantial amount. Planters will never pay that, even though it's categorically mentioned in the contract.'

'Someone has to foot that bill. Why not demand the cost for our return to the motherland from the independent India? The Chinese did it. As soon as Chinese labourers sign contracts, the return passage money is paid in advance. Madeirans get it, too. The Black man's story is different. They want to stay here, not return to Africa. Much like the Blacks, you Indians also want to stay in this country. You don't want to return to India,' Budho Singh concludes in a somber voice.

His words carry a heavy truth. Almost everyone who came to Guyana claimed to be of a noble Muslim or Brahmin status. Only a few of the untouchables boarded the ships. True or not, every Guyanese Indian clings to this belief. But upon returning to India, their past caste and identity, their so-called nobility, will definitely resurface. Will they accept the caste differences between them and their relatives? Caste segregation exists in Guyana as well, but it's only among the races, not within the races. As long as someone is Indian, there is no question about whether he or she is a Hindu, Muslim, Brahmin, or Kayastha. They are just one clan, one jaat.

Despite the rising tensions, they stand united as an Indian caste, a cohesive clan. Another factor is the promising future that Guyana holds for them. It doesn't matter if the terrain is a bit rough around the edges. Can India guarantee such a future? Returning home involves a hefty cost, and very few people have ventured to return to their homeland. Their savings rarely surpass two hundred dollars, a meagre sum considering a decade of hard-earned wages. Clinging to the soil of this country seems like a wise choice. This is why most are reluctant to risk their hard-earned capital on an uncertain gamble back in India.

After gaining freedom from the plantation, one can invest in land and venture into farming at his own will. Some of them have migrated to Georgetown, initiating small trading businesses. Fortune might favour some in such enterprises. Others are exploring opportunities to acquire paddy land and engage in cultivation. Guyana has lacked rice for the last fifty years, but now paddy fields on the south coast are yielding rice abundantly. Many liberated Indians have resettled in those regions, venturing into rice cultivation.

'Why not return to the paddy fields?' Lakshya Singh countered Budho Singh.

'Sure, I will return to my motherland and bow down to *Bharat mata* (mother India), undoubtedly,' Budho Singh asserts proudly. 'After four years and three months of slavery, my contract will expire. I will return to my Bharat mata and bow my head to my soil. The planter will cover the cost as per the signed contract. No need to dip into my savings.'

Budho Singh's pride is well-founded. He arrived in Guyana in 1901, when the demand for Indian labour was surging in Mauritius, the West Indies, and Trinidad. Amidst fierce competition, Budho Singh, with some education under his belt, negotiated favourable terms under the stringent contract imposed by the Guyanese planter.

'But what about Kanak Kumari?' Nakfal sneered, posing a sarcastic question.

'I am amassing shillings, not just silver. Kanak Kumari will return to our Bharat mata with me, where she will be the senior wife of our household,' Budho Singh declares with self-worth.

Kanak Kumari feels nervous. She would not like to leave her father and two sisters in the remote land of Guyana.

Kanak Kumari's heart quivered with trepidation as she observed the two Sahibs approaching, and she hastily veiled her head with the trailing end of her sari. She cast a sidelong glance at Budho Singh, who wore a grave expression. Does it signify the Sahib's wrath? A wave of tremour swept over Kanak Kumari.

Meanwhile, Nakfal remained audacious. He believed he had committed no wrong. In his opinion, Budho Singh was a fool for seeking justice. George Beauford would surely recognise Nakfal's loyalty as a committed driver. Unperturbed by the ethnic disparities, he always treated all labourers equally, for he was the band of the law.

George quickly glanced at his friend.

'I assume, in steering the ships, you mustn't have forgotten the labour laws dictated by the British company,' George remarked.

'Of course not. I can recall a few, at the very least,' Edward Jenkins assures him.

'In that case, you shall be the Judge today. It promises to be a novel experience,' George replied, nonchalantly reigniting his pipe.

'It would be my pleasure,' Edward responded.

He beckoned Nakfal closer.

All Indian labourers formed a circle on the ground; segregation was enforced to prevent different ethnicities from mingling. Death rituals in the Black man's household were of no interest at the moment; the Indian labourers were engrossed in Budho Singh's trial.

Nakfal presented his statement to the Sahib. He claimed to have received no orders from Master George regarding Kanak Kumari's release from work.

'Did you inform George when Kanak Kumari arrived at the plantation?' Edward inquired.

Nakfal shook his head, deeming it unnecessary to inform.

'Why not?' questioned Edward.

Nakfal explained that George had entrusted him with the full responsibility of the Indian labourers. George nodded in concurrence.

'Nakfal should have brought it to your knowledge, Sahib,' Budho Singh interjected, 'Kanak Kumari is not an indentured labourer; she moved to this plantation as a free woman.'

'Is that true?' Edward queried Nakfal.

Nakfal bowed his head in admission. There was no separate agreement with Kanak Kumari to work on George's plantation.

George Beauford now spoke up.

'This is absurd. No one can reside on my plantation without a contract. I should have been informed. You are at fault, Nakfal.'

'Not only that. He insulted my wife, harassed her, and forcibly took her to the Creole group for work. Kanak has not been listed in the ledger book,' Budho Singh attempted to incite him.

'Forced labour without a contract is illegal. Not permitted by British law,' Edward asserted.

'No, sir, I didn't force her to join the Creole group for work at the plantations. Please, ask the girls assembled here. Kanak Kumari went on her own accord,' Nakfal defended himself.

The gathered men and women nodded their heads with hushed giggles.

'Well, that's obviously not illegal,' Edward commented. 'As long as she is an adult, she has the right to go wherever she pleases.'

'I concur, sir,' Nakfal said, putting his hands together in the hope of a positive outcome. 'I did not force anything on Kanak Kumari. Sir, I only cared for Sahib's profits; I wanted to minimise his loss.'

'But I must find out the truth directly from her. Kanak Kumari, please stand up and step forward,' Edward ordered.

Kanak Kumari approached with her head bowed and eyes fixated on the ground, the veil drawn wide. She tried to squat on the ground, but Edward, disdainful of such postures, demanded she stand and speak.

'No, stand up and speak,' Edward Jenkins insisted, harbouring a bitter aversion to those African girls who squatted on the deck of slave ship with eyes constantly scanning the blue skies of the Atlantic. The Captain of the ship wished to spare himself from witnessing the pain of the girls. Moreover, Kanak Kumari's standing posture would not evoke sympathy from him—her sad looks would fall distant and unheeded against the backdrop of the blue trees and their blossoms.

'Remove the head scarf,' orders Edward, 'look straight in my eye.'

Kanak Kumari raised her gaze and met his inquisitive eyes.

'I want to learn the truth from you. If you lie, there will be severe consequences. Do you understand?' Edward warned Kanak Kumari.

She nodded in acknowledgement.

'Did driver Nakfal harass you?'

Kanak Kumari blushed, hesitant to respond. She mutely nodded.

'I need verbal confirmation. Do not shake your head.'

'Yes, he pestered me,' Kanak Kumari muttered softly.

'Can you elaborate on how he pestered you?'

'When everyone went to work in the sugarcane fields, Nakfal would discreetly come during the lunch break and knock on my door. He wanted to enter my cabin at the range. I had to stay indoors in fear with the door shut.'

'Did he insist? Did he try to break the door?'

'No, sir. But he used to coax a lot. He begged me to open the door and pleaded a lot.'

'What were the intentions of those talks?'

'I can't utter it, sir. I am very embarrassed,' Kanak Kumari confessed softly.

'Your husband has sought justice against Nakfal, the driver of the sugar company. He holds an administrative position in the company. Now is not the time to conceal the truth. You have to speak up. Come on, say it.'

Budho Singh encouraged her, 'Speak, Kanak Kumari. Tell everything. There's no reason for shame. You will be heard.'

Kanak Kumari opened her mouth tardily.

'He vowed to give me a nose ring made of gold and a gold chain. While Budho Singh gave me a silver nose ring and necklace, Nakfal claimed he would provide them in gold. He also promised that he would build a new house for me, next to Sahib's bungalow.'

Upon hearing this, the whole assembly of women, children, and the elderly erupted into roaring laughter. Edward Jenkins sharply scolded the unruly crowd.

'Silence! Silence, please! The trial is underway. Let me hear her. In what other ways did Nakfal Singh bother you?'

'In the morning, while trekking to the fields, he insisted on walking alongside me. No matter how many times I asked him not to, he wouldn't budge. He kept himself uncomfortably close to my body.'

Kanak Kumari admitted, her embarrassment evident. The crowd once again burst into a fit of laughter.

Latrines made their way to the plantations only in 1910. There were none until 1907. Whenever nature called, everyone had to go out—whether in rain, sun, or storm—across an expanse of two football fields. The girls had to visit quite early in the morning, before sunrise, or late at night after the master's roll call was over.

Sensing her shame, Edward Jenkins switched the topic. 'So, have you joined the Creole group on your own will? Did you go to the field?'

'Yes, I did, master.'

'Did Nakfal Singh force you to go?'

'No, sir. At first, I went willingly. But later, I didn't like it anymore. Then Nakfal forced me. Budho Singh wasn't around for more than a week, and I was scared.'

'Why did you refrain later?'

'Nakfal hit me with a cutlass,' Kanak Kumari said in fury.

'Cutlass!' Jenkins was taken aback. 'The large knife for cutting sugarcane? That sharp, curved knife?' he clarified.

'Yes, master. He flung it at me. I was badly cut, bleeding a lot.' Kanak Kumari's eyes filled with anguish.

'Why did Nakfal Singh throw the cutlass at you?'

'Because I couldn't slice the sugarcane properly. He said I caused a big loss to the company. How could I, master? I've never learned it. Nakfal didn't teach me; I could have learned it properly in a few days, master.'

'Let me check the wound. Where were you hurt?' Edward investigated.

Blushing again, Kanak Kumari pointed to the place where she was hurt—above the knee, close to the groin, and below the hip.

'I must see the wound. I need to make sure you're not

lying, and that you are speaking the truth. Now pull up your skirt; show me where the wound is.'

Kanak Kumari looked at him with wary eyes. If she were to lift her sari in front of the entire community, she would have to expose her vulnerability and cast off her shame. Her eyes turned bloodshot as she hesitated.

Edward insisted in English, 'I must see the bleeding wound, Kanak Kumari.'

Slowly, she pulled the saree up from her heels, revealing her beautifully-shaped thighs. No lies here. A bloody injury was clearly visible, three inches long; the blood just dried up and turned black.

'That's enough. You may sit down now, Kanak Kumari,' Edward ordered.

'Now, Nakfal Singh, step forward. It's your turn.'

Nakfal stepped forward, grinning.

'Budho Singh has brought up two grievous charges against you. The first charge is that you forced Kanak Kumari into the Creole group and made her work with them in the field. The trial revealed that Kanak Kumari went to the field of her own free will. Later, she did not want to go because of the pain in her thigh. You have all the rights to discipline a labourer during work. Hence, it's not a crime. Therefore, I acquit you of the first charge.'

Budho Singh's eyes darkened. The elders were correct. The Bukra trial is a farce; Bukra never knew how to judge.

'The other charge is that you have irritated Kanak

Kumari. I found out in court that you didn't just annoy her; you harassed her, showing temptation. The Penal Code of the Sugar Company clearly states that attempts for seducing someone else's wife or daughter is a serious offence. I find you guilty of that crime.'

Budho Singh's face brightened immediately. Who says the Bukra trial is a farce? Nakfal's punishment is coming. The verdict will be delivered right away.

'For your crime, the company will deduct one day's salary from your account,' Edward Jenkins announced in his verdict.

On their way back, Edward declared, 'Isn't she a rare beauty? Oh, my God, those bulky hips! God must have shaped them up with his own hands.'

With a subtle smile, George Beauford asked, 'Do you desire her?'

Taking a long drag from his pipe, Edward asks, 'Would that be proper?'

Edward was horrified yet curious.

'There is nothing improper on my plantation,' George Beauford announced proudly.

Nakfal himself extended the invitation to her with a delicate smile gracing his lips, 'Edward Sahib invites you to a dinner, Kanak Kumari! Fortune has smiled upon you. You have garnered the attention of the top boss, the master.'

There lies the crux of it. We're drawn to power, and emotions thrive in wealth. The planter has both power and wealth. Hence, everyone aligns with him—the Magistrate, the police, even the Governor. Planters command the highest standing in Guyanese society. They've always viewed plantation girls as their property. Whenever desire struck, they summoned them, indulged, and then callously discarded them like trash. However, the planter couldn't play openly with their desirable girls. Though secret attempts were made, they often met with minimal success. While some women eagerly sought the planter's favour, the majority consistently dodged his attention.

'Impossible!' hissed Budho Singh. 'Have you no integrity? You betrayed me once. And now you want to do the same with our community? Didn't you think twice before involving Kanak Kumari? Now, for the master's profit, you're again betraying us.'

'You're accusing me unjustly. I never spoke a word. Mr George Beauford himself called and asked me. Budho Singh, would you defy the master's orders?'

'Why would Beauford suddenly send for her?' Budho Singh argued. 'I've known him for years. His inclination is towards Black girls. His preference lies with Madeiran girls. Mr George has never shown interest in Indian girls. Why the sudden change today? You must have said something. Now you're concocting stories. I will not allow this to happen.'

Nakfal lowered his voice.

'Budho Singh, you're creating a fuss in the

neighbourhood for no reason. What's the benefit of escalating the commotion? You brought yourself to this perilous point by seeking judgement from a Bukra. Kanak Kumari has captured Edward's attention.'

Nakfal, too, finds things escalating quickly. Never in his wildest dreams did he imagine that Kanak Kumari would grab the admiration of Edward Sahib. Internal conflicts, even murder among themselves, were domestic matters. Now, the Sahib had entered the scene. If the word goes out, Indian society might believe it's Nakfal's manipulation—a revenge plot to secretly gift Kanak Kumari to the Sahib. If it spreads across Guyana, Nakfal himself will be discredited.

'Kanak Kumari will not leave my house at all.'

'What will I tell the Sahib?'

'Tell him exactly what I've said. The Sahib has no claim over Kanak Kumari.'

'This defiance will either cost me my job, or yours. We both could be fired.'

'Whichever, I am going to leave this place for good. I wish I had the opportunity to quit. But must I send over my bride to satisfy the master? Not at all.'

Nakfal tries to persuade him.

'The Sahib only invited Kanak Kumari for a meal. He didn't ask her to go to the bungalow; he didn't even request her to spend the night there. Why are you making a fuss, Budho Singh? Just ask Kanak Kumari to come with me and have her supper with the Sahib. I will escort her myself. The matter would be resolved. If you comply, George would be grateful enough to promote you with a job as a driver.'

'Are you ready to sacrifice your own driver's job for me? You really are such a benevolent friend!' Budho Singh remarks sarcastically.

'Not really. Someone shot dead a Black man driver the other day, and now that position is vacant. You may grab it.'

Budho Singh was stunned at hearing this, contemplating the odds.

'Never. I will not sacrifice my wife for a driver's job,' he gently utters after a while.

'Going against Sahib's orders, breaking discipline—George would never tolerate that.'

Discipline is like a chain; if broken once, it will set off a chain reaction. Discipline is the infallible principle of the plantation. No one is exempt from the grip of unwritten discipline, be it a rising gentleman overseer or the teenage daughter of a washing maid who has just entered puberty. Whoever stays on the plantation must obey the discipline. Discipline-breakers must be punished. But that discipline is not written anywhere; it is the pleasure of the planter, the owner. An Indian overseer complained that the planter would wake him up deep into the night and send him out ten miles away just to inspect whether the sluice gate had been closed the previous evening. If not, the morning tide would flood the plantation. Despite sheer exhaustion, the overseer would have to get out of his bed, forcing himself to get the horse out of the stable. He would walk ten miles on a cold night just to ensure the sluice gate was properly shut. There is no way to hide or misguide the planter; he had his eyes everywhere. The next morning, he would check with the gatekeeper to confirm if the overseer had truly come during the night. The planter, well aware that the sluice gate was closed, did this to assert his authority and discipline the overseer. George Beauford adeptly employed such measures.

'Summon Black man, Jesse Cook. Budho Singh will be subjected to punishment tomorrow morning in front of everyone. There will be flogging.'

Flogging is the perfect weapon in the planter's hand. Flogging in public is the punishment coolie labourers deserve for even the slightest mistake. One uniquely qualified person has been appointed on each plantation to conduct the flogging; the job is to strike the punished worker, making him stand bare chested in the hot sun, until he faints. Any able man drops after fifty strikes, faints after one hundred strikes, and certainly dies on receiving one hundred and fifty strikes. After one hundred floggings, Jesse Cook had never seen anyone come out with a steady life. However, death under these circumstances was not a crime in the eyes of British law.

'Tell him to deliver ten strikes at a time,' George

Beauford orders. 'And, he will continue until Budho Singh consents to my invitation.'

Nakfal acknowledges it with a nod. As he prepares to leave, George Beauford calls him back for further instructions.

'Instruct the Black man to apply salt to the wounds after caning. No water for the tongue. Strictly adhere to these directives.'

The flogging would be held under the crimson branches of the amaryllis tree. It is a public display of power. Everyone in society must attend the flogging on the planter's order. They must sit in a circle, gazing at the façade, the manifestation, and the demonstration of power.

The flogging commenced as soon as the golden sun began to brighten up the vast azure sky. Budho Singh took a squatting posture, face pressed down, exposing his back. Stripped and bound, legs to shoulders, a brick supported his clenched fist, his head bowed. The lashes commenced.

Kanak Kumari covered her ears. With each strike on Budho Singh, her body convulsed in unbearable pain, as if the whip were cutting through her soft flesh. Her screams echoed, 'No more, no more, no more.'

Yet, Budho Singh remained resolute and unyielding, like a rock! The lashes continued to rain upon him, but he kept his lips tightly sealed. No words escaped, and no signs of pain visible on his face.

After twenty strikes, Cook paused, questioning, 'Will

you accept Sahib's words?'

Budho Singh shook his head defiantly and said, 'No, no, no!'

Jesse Cook sprinkled the purple salt on his wounds, resumed the flogging, and halted again after fifty strikes, asking, 'Will you obey Sahib's order?'

Budho Singh replied with a single expression, 'No.'

More salt was sprinkled on the wounds, and the caning persisted. Fifty, sixty, seventy, and a hundred.

Kanak Kumari lost count. Her beautiful body now bore the shades of blue from pain; her nerves quivered, and her back, arms, and legs weighed heavy with agony. The mingling of saltwater and blood delivered a bitter, strange pain.

'One hundred and twenty! How much more can you endure, Budho Singh?' Cook, exhausted and panting, implored, 'Obey the Master.'

Budho Singh shook his head resolutely and said, 'No, I won't accept.'

One hundred thirty, one hundred forty, one hundred fifty—the flogging persisted. Jesse Cook, fatigued and panting, asked again, 'Accept it, Budho Singh.'

Cook's heart began to soften. In all his years of administering canings, he had never seen an Indian endure so many lashes at once. Black men could endure, but even they weakened after seventy-eight strikes. He was convinced that a few more lashes would surely prove fatal for Budho Singh. Gurgling, almost on the brink of death, as life resurged within him, Budho Singh vehemently declared, 'No, no, no!'

One hundred sixty, one hundred sixty-one, one hundred sixty-two...

Kanak Kumari could not bear the pain any longer. Her body, now bruised blue, descended from the threshold. Kanak Kumari stared at Nakfal. She was ready to go to Sahib, ready to face the fire and even death.

That night, Edward Jenkins adorned the dinner table with candlelight, and gazed long at Kanak Kumari with enchanted eyes.

***

'Why did Budho Singh escape death that day?' Mohon Singh was abuzz with anger. 'Why didn't he meet his end? If he had, I wouldn't be the talk of the town today. Budho Singh, why didn't you meet your demise? Why did you surrender to Kanak Kumari's ploy to keep you alive so that she could enjoy her life unashamedly? Why did you welcome Kanak Kumari back to your home? Why not cast that tainted woman away?' Mohon Singh's voice echoed with a multitude of questions, like a raging lion in captivity.

'Master, what are you doing? Pay heed! Are you napping?' Amoz Rangeela screamed from the back.

Mohon Singh jerked back to reality. It was evident

that the vehemence of his anger had transferred to the DC-3 engine. Abruptly stopping, it swooped down. In a few seconds, the plane's nose would collide straight into the hill. Lives would be shattered, and a gruesome accident loomed.

Mohon Singh contemplated his options. Should he not restrain the plane's momentum? Should he not dive down the hills and shut the very veins that channeled black blood clots to the wombs of Indo-Guyanese women? Mohon resolves, from now on, no Indo-Guyanese women would be seeded by a blood clot stained by black blood.

In a mad dash, Mohon adjusted the aerodynamics and rocketed the plane up into the sky. The regret lingered in his mind. A profound ache gripped his heart. Mohon couldn't shake it off, nor could he embrace it.

Chapter Five

The Cereus Flower

'Maa, you were right,' Shovon sits beside his mother, burying his face in her lap like a child, 'It was my mistake.'

Paromita, startled by this sudden affectionate call, gently pats his dried hair and asks, 'Don't you apply oil to your hair anymore? It's a mess! Doesn't your wife notice?'

'You're still an old-fashioned lady, Maa. Nowadays, nobody oils their hair like my dad. Won't it stick to the head? The hair should remain free, flowing with the light breeze,' Shovon smiles.

'But I like your father's neat hair with cream,' Paromita replies with a smile. 'Now, tell me, what you want to say, Beta.'

'Maa, I want to marry Rania,' Shovon smilingly utters.

'That's great news, my dear *babu*. Your Baba will be delighted to hear this news. He's been longing to embrace his grandson. But every time he draws him near, his heart wavers, conflicted by his religious beliefs.'

'You're right, Maa. I've seen Baba holding Tony lovingly, drawing him near his chest, bringing him close to his heart, but suddenly Baba pushes Tony away and retracts immediately. Rania says, "Dad hates Tony,"' Shovon acknowledges.

'No, Shovon, our blood flows through his veins, Tony is a descendant of Rehman Majeed. Could your father ever hate him?' Paromita endeavours to shield Rehman from undue blame.

'He's obsessed with Tony, incessantly talking about him—where and how he would complete his education. Baba plans to send Tony to a boarding school to study with the British boys, and he'll return as a Barrister from London. Tony will join Cheddi Jagan's practice.' Paromita reveals Rehman's treasured secret to her son.

'Boarding schools would be quite expensive. Will Baba provide the necessary funds?' Shovon inquires.

'Absolutely, he said he'd do it a hundred times. He plans to bring four more cabs next year. Then we won't have to worry anymore. Whatever we earn, we'll lead a comfortable life. Your wedding will definitely incur some costs. But then, it's the marriage of our only son—shouldn't the event be grand? Bells will chime, stars will shine, and all the bungalows will sparkle with light,' Paromita says smiling. 'These days, they're capturing moments on cinema camera like Bollywood films; we'll also capture all the events of your wedding.'

'Maa, something's amiss,' Shovon hesitates and finally reveals, 'It's only me who wants to get married. Rania doesn't agree with me.'

'Why? What does she say?' Paromita is surprised now and more eager to understand. Historically, boys have seldom been keen on marriage, whereas girls are almost always interested. Why is Rania defying the natural order?

***

In the end, Paromita makes it to Rania's room. She rarely wanders into this wing of her large mansion, even less so since Rania's arrival. Designed by an architect, the two-storey bungalow-type house fulfills Paromita's two demands—rare architectural beauty and absolute privacy. When Shovon and Reeta would get married, and their future grandchildren form a close-knit family, every part of the house would ensure adequate privacy. Paromita didn't want her children to leave the house due to space and privacy constraints. The architects planned accordingly and succeeded in creating a balanced home. On the rear side, below, Reeta resides with Mohon Singh, leading their own way of life. Yet, they step into their parent's quarters whenever they want to, spending a few evenings or afternoons in joy.

It's 11 am. Rania is sleeping in bed, Western music blaring from the stereo. The ears are bombarded with intense beats. Rania is lying with her eyes closed, absorbing the music. Paromita wonders how anyone can comfortably doze amidst such loud noise.

'Rania, may I come in?' Paromita knocks on the door.

Rania takes a moment to unwind from her inertia. Upon seeing Paromita, she hurriedly composes herself. She was dressed in a black nightie that gracefully covered her golden, sun-kissed skin, and had straight, snake-like curls and a bored expression. Paromita reflects in her mind. Rania is undoubtedly beautiful. She has inherited the bright, sun-burnt golden texture of the Madeirans. She would look stunning in a red *Banarasi* saree as a bride.

'Please, come in, Mrs Majeed,' Rania calls out. 'I'm going to change my clothes right away.'

'Oh no, dear, you don't have to be formal. It's nothing serious. I just came to have a word with you.'

'I am flattered, Mrs Majeed.'

Rania lowers the volume of the stereo, takes out a white shawl, drapes herself, and settles next to Paromita. 'I am all ears, Mrs Majeed.'

Rania never addresses her as a mother. She grieves this. She reminisces about the blue-eyed bride, Janet, and how respectfully she sat. The moment Bachaoni entered the room, she prostrated and touched the elders' feet. She knelt down to kiss all the little ones. She addressed her mother-in-law as Mataji with a strange emotion. Perhaps, Rania will do the same when she gets married. She is still the daughter of a Madeiran family, and that is why she is so formal. Paromita holds hope close to her heart.

'Up so late?' Paromita queries with a smile.

'We had a party last night and we returned late. Shovon says it was almost early morning by then. He claims he even heard the birds singing. But I didn't hear anything. My ears were plugged in sleep.'

'What time was it? Did you check the watch?'

'I never carry a wristwatch to a party,' Rania declares without a blink. 'Why bring a watch when you're going to a party? When I'm happy, I don't want the constraints of time deflect me, Mrs Majeed. I'll stay as long as I want to savour the moment. I'll leave when the itch fades.'

'I've heard you have these parties almost every other night!' Paromita articulates, combining sorrow with a smile.

'We do. But not all of them are equally thrilling. Some parties are really good. Shovon occasionally lingers at the party, just to keep up the formality. But I don't agree. I say it's far better to go home, lie in bed, and listen to jazz. Should I turn up the volume of the stereo, Mrs Majeed? Do you like it?'

'Go ahead, if you want to.'

'I'm sorry, I don't have any Indian music cassettes. Shovon had a few, but I can't say where they are kept now since I haven't heard them lately. So, what music should I put on? Classical? Let's see if I can find anything,' Rania becomes distraught.

'I did not come to listen to music, Rania. I just wanted to talk to you. You better come near me, and sit next to me.'

Rania gets up from the front sofa and sits next to Paromita, raising her eager eyes. 'Tell me, Mrs Majeed.'

'Shovon says he wants to get married, but you don't agree to his proposal.'

Rania bows her head and thinks for a while. 'Yeah, Mrs Majeed, I told him, "What is the benefit of performing the social formality?" We're doing well already. Why tighten our conjugal bond with a legal matrimonial tie?'

'Marriage is the secure base of life. It is a foundation of a perpetual family bond. Why do you think it is simply a legal tie?' Paromita wants to know.

'I will have to follow lots of rules when I get married,' Rania states clearly. 'The customs of your Indian society are very complex, may be some of those are pointless. Shovon will then force me to accept and adhere to those rites.'

Paromita is startled by this unexpected revelation. Had Rania subtly vented a disdain for the coolies? Do those eyes harbour hatred for the clan of coolies? The Portuguese consider themselves a proud nation, believing in their equality with the Europeans. Madeirans, in their pride, never give tips directly into the hands of the Indian coolies; they would instead throw them on the ground. The eager, yet greedy, Indian coolie would then pick up the coins with a sense of self-satisfaction. Did Rania's words evoke a reminder of the age-old animosity in Paromita mind?

'Shovon is a very elegant young man. He will never insist on imposing customs that you personally find disagreeable. I assure you, nor will we.'

'I trust you won't. But in Indian society, rumours can spread swiftly. This community is quite gossipy. And at times, you might grow tired of hearing those relentless gossips about us. Then, in the name of family honour and the institution of marriage, there may be interference with our personal freedom.'

'So, Rania, it's not that you fear the institution of marriage itself? Rather, you fear how we might treat you after your formal marriage.'

'I fear both. I cherish my freedom now. Marriage, in my perception, could jeopardise that freedom. Later, I might find myself living in complete subjugation.'

'Your perspective is not entirely accurate. Marriage has the potential to bring fulfillment and satisfaction.'

'I am now thoroughly content, Mrs Majeed.'

'Your satisfaction is noted. But, what about Shovon? Won't you like to see him happy as well?' Paromita inquires with a subtle hint of annoyance.

'Shovon creates shifting images of himself routinely. Now, he pictures himself adorning an *achkan*, donning a *pugree,* turban atop his head, making a grand entrance at the wedding ceremony on a white horse, while I would be adorned in a red Banarasi saree imported from Calcutta. I would have to endure hours amidst the commotion of the wedding festivities, draped in those vibrant colors. It's absurd!'

Rania softly expresses her perspective on the Indo-Guyanese rites of marriage. Paromita finds herself recalling the words of the blue-eyed bride. It has been a while since Janet Jagan's last visit. She is now the Minister of Home Affairs. Paromita resolves that she must reach out to Janet and talk. Janet, not native to Guyana, did not dislike Guyanese society. Instead, she wholeheartedly embraced Guyana's culture. The customs that seemed questionable to her were not discarded out of disdain. Instead, for Guyana's rights, Janet relinquished the most precious privilege of her life—her citizenship. By organising relentless freedom movements and participating in Guyana's 1950 elections, she sacrificed her birthright and her US citizenship. And Rania? Though born and raised in Guyana, she harbours animosity towards a significant segment of Guyanese society. If Rania truly despises the Indo-Guyanese customs, why has she entangled herself with Shovon Majeed? Why did she not trap a partner from her own community and clan? Paromita looks for ways to understand Rania better.

'But, do you believe a church wedding would be more agreeable to you? Are you open to the idea of getting married in a church?'

Rania remains silent for a while. Eventually, she responds, 'I am not assured Mrs Majeed.'

Paromita exits her room.

***

Assurance—does it ever materialise? Yet, what assurance did Cheddi Jagan provide to Janet? What conviction prompted Janet to leave her country with just one dollar in hand? Was it the determination shining fiercely in Cheddi Jagan's bright eyes that inspired Janet to plunge into the intense politics of Guyana?

It seems the words from three women are continually whispering into the ears of a distraught Paromita, leaving an indelible imprint on her future. The first whisper is Bachaoni Jagan's, who has been driven by the desire to educate her children to their fullest potential as a means of escaping poverty. The second whisper is from Janet Jagan, who harboured aspirations for women's emancipation and Guyana's freedom from imperial rules. And now, Rania is whispering her desire to be liberated from the constraints of Indian customs for her own emancipation. All the three women are seeking emancipation through separate, but distinct, quests within the soil of Guyana.

Paromita turns on the radio to hear BBC World News. The headline says that Janet Jagan, the Home Minster of Guyana, has resigned from the Cabinet protesting non-cooperation from her Guyana Police Forces, who are fully controlled by the colonial British. Paromita expresses a sigh of relief. Her mentor, Janet, will no longer be a victim of unfound gossips.

For how long could a romantic girl from an adversarial country endure constantly doubting rumours and disdains of the self-seekers since her arrival at her adopted land? Does her resignation signal that she would be retiring from the politics of Guyana? Paromita traces back her own precious moments with her mentor Janet.

Janet was a down to earth Guyanese housewife. She swept the house, cleansed the courtyard with a coating of cow dung, and engaged with neighbours in debates and discussion on various themes—politics, society, and revolution. Janet bathed the Afro-Guyanese babies in the outskirts of Georgetown, while encouraging the reluctant Black mothers to join her women's cooperatives.

Early in 1950s, Janet Jagan actively engaged with the Guyanese women, belonging to all races, serving and toiling within the interior of the walls, for their emancipation and acquiring their economic rights. Cheddi Jagan organised political assemblies for men beyond the confines of their residence. Janet harboured no disdain for the varied customs and practices of different creeds of Guyanese society and not even the conservative rites of the Indian society. If just a decade ago, a foreign-born fairy was untouched by those traditional constraints, then why, now in 1964, a native-born Guyanese woman named Rania openly expresses her disdain for the customs of her fellow creeds? How did such indifference take root in the heart of this young woman of her land? Could this be the seed of divisions between the six races that the British is creating to prolong the colonial rule till they discover oil on its sea shore? The British and the Americans are showing unusual interest in the upcoming elections. Rumours are spreading that America has decided to support Forbes Burnham. Prime Minister Wilson will prefer someone other than Cheddi Jagan, probabaly from the Indo-Guyanese community to lead the post-election government. Does the clarion call for freedom also lure the malevolence of corruption and malice, permeating through castes, colours, and races? Why this perplexity?

But Janet's strong organisation skill to form the first political party of Guyana, the People's Progressive Party (PPP) during 1950, caused envy among a few experienced political leaders. They were disgruntled that she became Office Secretary of the PPP. Hissed words spread that Janet's ascend to the spiral stairs of power was through scheming and manoeuvering. This conundrum emerged long ago, subjecting narrow-minded skeptics to spread unfounded gossips about Janet. Janet's arrival in Guyana was not to foster unity, but to sow the seed of discord. An outsider, Janet, often cast doubts on the relations between the Black and the Coolie, the Chinese and the Madeirans, the British and the Amerindians. It appeared that this woman is insatiably power-hungry. Abandoning her homeland, she sought refuge in Guyana for the sole purpose of attaining absolute power. A progeny of the Bukra, she unhesitatingly mingled and dined with the Amerindians, Chinese, Blacks and Portuguese; while her conservative Indians families still clung to shades of caste. Why is Janet loitering everywhere? Is it not solely for her lust for harnessing political power? Janet identifies herself with the coolies; only because Indians possess the capacity to propel the American lady forward, elevating her stature and honour. Blacks would never entertain such endeavours; neither would any man of other races. Did Janet has ensnared the Indians with her insatiable hunger for ascension to power?

The critics forget that the solemn journey of Janet Jagan under the leadership of Cheddi Jagan commenced from the atrium of Port Mourant for snatching freedom from the reluctant imperial powers. Janet, flanked by Cheddi, spearheaded the organisation of a trade union, the PAC, which later enabled birthing the People's Progressive Party (PPP). They championed the cause of a thousand labourers, decrying the tyranny of the sugar plantations. Resistance must be faced head-on; progress must be made, initiating the struggle for freedom—a united claim of six races. Coolies' pay should be increased, profits should be allocated fairly, and the ranges' bus system needs to be improved. Plantations owners have more obligations to perform and varied duties to carry out at the plantations, such as supplying food, clothing, and educational materials. Failure to comply will incite a hunger strike. Janet queried 'For how long, under the scorching Caribbean sun, beads of sweat and droplets of blood trickle down the weary coolies' hearts?'

Cheddi shouted to the crowds, 'The Bukra must reckon the cost of that blood.'

Plantation owners under the patronage of colonial rulers remained unmoved and unnerved. In 1948, the village Enmore witnessed spilling of innocent blood—neither a Black's, nor a labourer's, but in fact, the blood of six subjugated races. The funeral procession marched from Enmore to Georgetown, spanning a formidable sixteen miles. A multitude of coolies, a myriad of labourers, an assembly of farmers, men, women and children, walked hand in hand—where the demise of one labourer resonated as the demise of a million. Alongside the Black leader Forbes Burnham and Aguilar, leader of the Portuguese, Cheddi Jagan and Janet Jagan spearheaded the march, all affected by the tapestry of Guyanese society. Six nations marched forward united—where was the schism in those olden days? The funeral march, a manifestation of unity, progressed hand in hand, resonating with anthems and echoing calls for an unyielding revolution, 'In life, we are unified; in death, we perish collectively.'

***

Paromita assigned Reeta the task of executing her son's wishes.

'I can't comprehend the girl, Reeta. Does Rania detest Indians, given her reluctance to marry Shovon? If she is so unwilling, why is she clinging to Shovon as her partner? He is also Indian. Why not let him go? We can arrange his marriage with another girl.'

Reeta was reluctant to accept the assignment. She replied, 'No, Maa. You must have misunderstood her.'

'Perhaps you are correct. We are from a different era. I struggle to grasp the ways and values of your generation. Now, please help me understand Rania; go and converse with her; try to fathom the dilemma creeping in her mind.'

Reeta enters Rania's room, where she is welcomed with a smile.

'Shovon must have initiated a massive campaign within the family. First, Mrs Majeed visited, and now you are here. I am sure Mohon will be next; may be even Mr Rehman Majeed will invite me formally to meet him over a cup of tea. I doubt he will himself come to this wing of his home. He is a proud man, and I am utterly unacceptable to him.'

'Not at all, Rania. Baba misses Tony greatly.'

'I don't deny it. But every time Mr Majeed sees me, his eyes boil with anger. I can't endure the intensity of his gaze.'

'My father's gaze is sharp. Nothing can be concealed from him. He would expose it with just a glance. I understand your fear, your uneasiness,' Reeta acknowledges.

'I'm scared even to go near him and greet him!' Rania confesses.

'From a distance, Baba may look intimidating, but if you come near to him, you'll find Baba indeed holds a gentle soul.'

'I won't dare to verify that fact. I am apprehensive. I am fearful.'

'You are letting fear fester in your mind, Rania.'

'Yes, and that's why I resist what Shovon is proposing.'

'Is it solely about the fear of marriage? I have been through this process. Suspicions, disturbances—everything came to my mind, but I did not succumb to fear.'

'I get it. My fear is about change. Why disrupt the flow when things are going smoothly?'

'But it's not stable. If neither of you wishes to marry, I would understand that there's an agreement between you.'

'There was a stability of thoughts between us. But, nowadays, Shovon wants the opposite.'

'So, you two are on different wave lengths now.'

'I certainly agree with that,' Rania proudly asserts, picking up words from Reeta and boldly stating, 'Shovon keeps proposing to me every evening at every party; he promises to adorn me with a gold wedding crown, ala Indian style.'

'But how can you dismiss Shovon's headway?' Reeta inquires, surprised.

'Perhaps, I'm extraordinary!' Rania responds with a content smile. 'That's probably my biggest allure—to be able to captivate and resist Shovon.'

'I've missed your point, Rania!'

'Shovon loves me. He wants to fulfill my every desire. He addresses every concern of mine with his own passion. He's a wonderful man,' Rania extols Shovon.

'Do you truly feel that, Rania?'

'Absolutely.'

'But don't you fear the cost of turning down his desire every time he asks you?' Reeta asks, astonished.

'You may be misunderstanding me, Reeta. I don't want to marry Shovon simply because he's uniquely fascinated with me. I've witnessed many men profess love before marriage only to lay off their wives afterwards, brushing them off as mere spouses. Once a woman is bound by marriage, she becomes readily available and guaranteed, losing her allure to her man; unless she's like a fluttering butterfly.'

'Your words are perplexing, Rania.'

'They won't be perplexing at all. Rest your mind on it, Reeta. Go home and reflect. Compare the current impact of your charm on Mohon with its past. Only then you shall grasp my perspective,' Rania responds gently.

'Men seek possession. They want control of their possession. Women are their possession. The moment men achieve complete possession of the women they seek, at that very instance they lose their interest. His strong attraction towards that woman diminishes instantly.'

'Are you suggesting that Shovon's desire to marry you formally is merely a childish endeavour?' Reeta asks, annoyed.

'No, I see Shovon's desire as a perfect and pure reflection of his love for me. I don't want to lose it. I don't want to be just a wife. I aspire to be his own enchanting woman for eternity. If not as a wife, I'll exist as that unique woman in Shovon's eyes and heart. That will be his ultimate lure for me. It will be my greatest gift to him.'

With determination, Rania conveys her decision to Reeta.

Rehman couldn't believe his senses upon hearing the news—Rania's refusal to marry Shovon. As he regained his composure, fury coursed through him. How dare she defy the status of Rehman Majeed's daughter-in-law and thereby insult Shovon? That girl cannot coexist within the confines of his home. He summoned Shovon; Paromita too rushed in, fearing a battle between father and son.

'There's a snake nesting in the house, waiting for the right moment to strike. We will all perish, I will perish, and the entire Majeed family will be ruined. Rid yourselves of this snake as soon as possible.'

In an effort to reason with his father, Shovon said, 'You're blowing things out of proportion. It's a personal matter. We'll handle it. Don't complicate matters by meddling.'

'Meddling? Listen to the boy's words!' Rehman kept

growling in resentment. 'The little boy has now come of age. If you don't defy your father, how will you prove your worth to the Madeiran society? I wish well for my only son and, in return, my son blames me for insulting his lover!'

'Baba, no one is blaming you. Reconciling with Rania is my responsibility, not yours. You bear no responsibility,' Shovon explained.

'Of course, we have a responsibility. Why did you bring the Madeiran girl in our home? Were you not aware that Madeiran girls are betrayers? Historically unfaithful to their Indian husbands?'

'Father, you cannot generalise an entire caste based on the actions of a single girl in the past,' Shovon remained respectful but argued his point.

The incident took place thirty years ago, in 1934, between a Portuguese wife and an Indian husband. During a brawl, the wife impulsively stabbed her husband to death. Yet she faced no consequences, and escaped punishment under the British law. Consequently, conflict over caste identity arose, sparking a larger issue.

'I see doom approaching. Paromita was correct. More riots and murders are imminent. Guyana will descend into chaos. Cheddi Jagan succumbed to pressure from the Madeiran leader, Aguilar. This time, riots are inevitable. What will you do then?' Rehman persisted.

'Why do you keep bringing up the riots, Baba?' Shovon asked with a smile. 'Who were rioting on the streets of

Georgetown in July 1964? It was the middle-agers fooled by their respective aged political leaders. We, the young generations, were not participating in riots; we long for our future. Riots will not preserve our future. On the contrary, peaceful coexistence will enable us to move forward. Unlike your generation,we don't blindly believe in engaging in riots like your ancestors did in India by sparking Hindu-Muslim riots on the midnight of India's Independence. Why would we, the new generation, divide ourselves while marching forward to snatch our freedom from the colonials? On what grounds? For what faith? And for which skin colour?'

'The riots won't be about religion, but about caste and colour.'

'Impossible, Baba. We are not as emotionally charged as you are. Why should we ruin our country by killing each other; by nabbing our brothers and sisters with whom we grew up in our neighbourhoods? You see colours and caste, Baba! We see friends!' Shovon countered.

'Hasn't it already been ruined? Didn't the riots persist? Weren't the streets of Georgetown ablaze? Weren't men and women lying in pools of blood? Didn't the Blacks come from behind and knifed the innocent Indians?' Rehman bombarded him with a series of questions.

Shovon confronts his father's emotional assessment, 'Look at the facts, Baba! The Afro-Guyanese has not yet gained leadership and power in Guyana. They shared power under the leadership of the Indo-Guyanese. Cheddi Jagan began his ascend to power during 1953 and retained it till today, for 11 years. Throughout this period, 1953 to 1964, it is admirable that Burnham has remained a close friend of Cheddi, even though they charted their respective paths of political ideology. They were both school mates. Burham served faithfully as an effective Minister of Education under the Cheddi cabinet. Burnham was Mayor of Georgetown, while Jagan was the Premier of the country. But after a 11-years leadership, why are the senior Indo-Guyanese apprehensive that their political advantage could be compromised by the new decree of proportional representation in the upcoming elections? We, the youth, do not subscribe to PR apprehensions. We will remain united with other races.'

'Unless all the Indo-Guyanese, young and old, remain together during this election, we as an Indian race will be further weakened. We have none to align with, but ourselves. The Blacks will strike us if given the chance. Madeirans will deceive. I can't exempt the Chinese either. I am afraid, if my own son shifts his political support from his apni jaat, the family wealth I've amassed will vanish like the smoke of single lighted cigarette,' Rehman asserts.

Paromita gets puzzled at the turn of the tones between the father and son.

'This money is hard-earned, and comes with a lot of pain. But there's honour in my money. To earn this money, I didn't have to bribe authorities sending my wife, like many others. Or like the Madeirans, I didn't have to give away my daughter to the British. There was no need to pursue other women, like the Chinese. I've built this wealth with my own hands and my own sweat.'

'With your aging brain, you seem to be at a loss for correct words, Rehman. Speak up clearly what you have in your mind. Do not bring up irrelevant issues,' Paromita interjects with a tone of authority.

'What more is there to say?' Rehman declares without hesitation, 'There will be more bloodshed in Guyana. I am certain. If Shovon marries Rania, Madeiran rioters will intrude within our own house. The risks for my family will increase. It's better to rid ourselves of that girl.'

Paromita is taken aback. She never anticipated such reactionary words from Rehman Majeed.

'Do you understand your father's perspective, Shovon?' She gazes at Shovon, seeking clarity.

Shovon turns back to his distraught father with deep compassion.

'I am sorry, Baba! I am really unable to accept the hypocrisy existing in the Indo-Guyanese society. The reality of indentured workers' life in Guyana and the leaders of your community have enabled you to accommodate the rites of Hindu and Muslim faith within your community. No one from outside interfered with your decisions. I admire the advancement of your thoughts. But, you have failed to accommodate yourselves and your progenies with the God-given skin colours. We are growing together side by side, within proximities of our own neighbourhood, and yet we are continually warned by our parents that "Beware of the skin colour of your classmates, your work colleagues or your grocer." It is not the colonials who are dividing us; it is our prejudices that are restraining us.'

Rehman looks at his son, amazed. He has grown up. He is speaking up his thoughts, which may be painful to listen but carry far reaching values for his progenies.

'We are not the only exceptions, Shovon,' reasserts Rehman, but his voice sounds feeble. 'Blacks are staying within themselves; Amerindians had always been insular.'

'Why would they not be insular, Baba! They are minorities in their own land. We are the majority in a land, where the Blacks came first from Africa and then we came, voluntarily or involuntarily. Now, we are holding a marginal majority. We the Indo-Guyanese should take the lead to integrate our society for marching to the freedom of Guyana.'

'Cheddi is the first person who brought the entire Guyanese society together for the united march of freedom,' Rehman reminds his son.

'I agree, my march as a school boy was a united march. We, the youths, are still keeping with us the spirit of 1953. But your generation has not marched forward ever since with the same spirit! Have you ever thought why your generation have strayed?' Shovon asks his father directly.

Puzzled by the query, Rehman remains silent.

Shovon returns his sharp glance to his mother.

'Maa, I understand your predicament. But your son does not hold a choice. A girl has placed her trust on me! She loves me. I cannot trample her sacred trust fearing fictional rioters,' Shovon responds with a firm conviction.

***

On 31 October 1964, Duncan Sandys announces that the 1964 election will be held on the basis of proportional representation on 7 December 1964. The BBC World Service carries the news over the air. Hearing this, Rehman Majeed bursts in anger.

Cheddi Jagan objects to the new electoral system, but later decides to participate in the election. Rehman's expectations came alive within a week of Duncan Sandys' announcement of the 1964 election schedule. On a cloudy November morning of 1964, the Boeing 707 touched down on the airport tarmac. Rodriguez descended, hands raised in greeting, a bright smile adorning his bearded face. Majeed, having secured his clearance, joyfully ascended the stairs to warmly embrace his long-missed friend.

Rodriguez has resurfaced coincidentally after an extensive hiatus of nearly two years. Rehman Majeed, reflecting on his loyal customer of a decade, felt perturbed by his irregular visits to Guyana. Rehman had concerns about his illness or a shift in focus to another endeavour. All the unanswered inquiries stem from the want of Rodriguez's home address. So, despite feeling a bit uneasy, Rehman patiently waited. And yet Rodriguez remained elusive! It was an unprecedented instance in Guyana's history. Rehman noted that whenever dark political clouds shrouded Guyana's sky, his decade-long client Rodriguez showed up in Georgetown, sporting an air of awe.

'Where have you been for so long? You seem to have gained some weight and have grown a beard,' remarked Majeed.

'I was introspective, and now I have found myself,' Rodriguez chuckled.

'I don't quite understand,' perplexed, Rehman inquired.

'I sought solace in a monastery, contemplating and seeking answers to the myriad questions in my mind,' Rodriguez explained with a gentle smile.

'Have you found the answers for your restless mind?' Majeed inquired.

'Not for all the questions, but I've discovered the destiny of my future life; I've become an artist.'

Rodriguez unloaded a dozen wooden boxes, each containing artworks.

'Are all these your creations?' Majeed queried. 'If I had known earlier, I would have brought a pickup. Let me work on this now. What do you plan to do with so many paintings?'

'Some are mine; others belong either to Caribbean artists or to Cuban. I'm here to curate an exhibition. I'll extend invitations to everyone,' Rodriguez said, radiating enthusiasm. 'I will ask the media to meet this dedicated artist from USA.'

Rodriguez pulled off a flawless art exhibition, featuring ninety-seven paintings by a total of thirty-one artists, including thirteen of his own, held in a secluded area of the prestigious Clara Lodge. The exhibition, a month-long spectacle, unfolded seamlessly.

Rodriguez demonstrated astute political acumen, cleverly leveraging the pretext of an exhibition. Cheddi Jagan inaugurated the exhibition. Burnham graced the occasion as the Chief Guest, on condition that Forbes would also conclude the show. D'Aguilar, as the Chief Patron, hosted the reception dinner for the invited elites of Georgetown. Invigorating the campaigns of the United Front for the impending election served as the focal point of his welcoming speech. D'Aguilar elicited popularity from the gathered elites. In the interlude, Cuban artists warmly hosted Guyanese artists at a reception, fostering cultural exchange and camaraderie. The upcoming election intensified the warmth and energy stirred by the art exhibition, which had attracted Guyana's entire intellectual milieu. Groups of intellectuals, students, businessmen, and housewives transformed the artists' congregation into a jubilant festival.

Reeta walks towards her father as Rehman makes his way to the cab fleet depot. Following the announcement of national elections, the influx of foreigners into Guyana has surged, bringing journalists, businessmen, bankers, and international donors—Americans, Britons, Cubans, Romanians, and Russians. The once-forgotten Guyana is now bustling with activity. The election anticipated about 90 per cent of popular turnouts. Such a possible turnout has stirred up enthusiasm among young voters, brightening the prospect of a power shift. The Quit Guyana Movement against the British echoes all the way to Georgetown.

'Baba, I need to talk to you,' Reeta says, stepping closer.

Rehman wraps his hands around her and says, 'You've withdrawn yourself since your marriage. You hardly visit me.'

Reeta combs through her father's greying hair with her fingers. 'Can I tell you something without you getting angry again?'

'Do you only see anger in me?' Rehman feels hurt. 'Can't you see the limitless love I hold for you?'

'I am only here because I know it, Baba,' Reeta speaks softly.

'When I sent you to school, they all laughed and objected. They said, "Will Rehman Majeed make his girl a Christian by sending her to the school of the Church? You will lose her!" I didn't pay heed. I sent you and Shovon to elite schools. I did not send you to our traditional madarasa run by the Mosque. In those days, I didn't have much money. I had to struggle a lot to educate both of you, darling.'

'I know, Baba. Maa told us you worked from morning till night, sometimes beyond midnight.'

'Your mother used to wait for me, starving, by the flickering lamp. She was a seamstress once. I repeatedly pleaded with her not to stay up late working. I would tell her to eat and sleep, but she would not listen,' Rehman recalls.

'I remember, Baba,' Reeta also immerses in past memories. 'Sometimes, I couldn't sleep. I was afraid you wouldn't return. You may get caught in a riot somewhere. Maa was always worried! She would say riots and road blockades were happening all over Guyana. She would say secret killings were all around. I feared that someone mistakenly may stab you while you are returning late nights from the interiors carrying the foreign visitors in your cab. I would lie in bed with my eyes closed. You used to arrive late at night. My mother would reheat food. At that moment, you would come to me, sit on my bed, pull the blanket, and kiss me on my forehead. I would sleep happily, knowing that you had returned home. You know, Baba, sometimes I didn't see you for weeks because you would leave home early in the morning and return late at night. I would wait all day, anticipating that little kiss on my forehead during my sleep.'

Tears well up in Rehman's eyes. He tries to wipe

them away with a handkerchief and has an urge to embrace Reeta, reminiscent of her childhood times. However, he refrains.

'But what reward I got for my toil, Reeta? I find myself tending to a serpent thriving within our abode, wrestling with a bushmaster, more formidable than a jungle cobra.' Rehman reveals a heart filled with resentment.

'Don't be angry with Shovon, Baba. Rania is a very deserving girl. Soft heart, soft mind. She cannot harm us in any way.'

'I know she alone will not be able to do any harm to us. But what happens if there is a racial riot before the elections? D'Aguilar is delivering angry speeches. Which side will she take? Will she not seek shelter with her parents,' Rehman gets irritated. He didn't like Reeta taking Rania's side.

'Must she take a side, Baba?' Reeta inquires.

'In the moment of mass hysteria, she'll definitely be compelled to pick a side. In such moments, rational boundaries blur, and individuals, overcome with fervour, forge ahead. Would Rania not harbour a strong allegiance to her parents? Wouldn't her allegiance to her own ethnicity strongly influence her? Will she truly abandon them for us?'

'Perhaps she won't; she would possibly like to return to the Madeirans. But her parents have disowned her for marrying out of caste,' Reeta admits.

'But her mom reconciled, and baked cake for Shovon!' Rehman reminds.

'Why would Rania resort to a betrayal within our family? She has been welcomed by all of us.'

'She might not betray willingly, but circumstances could force her hand. Many Guyanese harbour jealousy towards me. They would revel in the discovery of a rift within Majeed family.'

'Baba, your hyper-concerns about a forthcoming racial riot appear unfounded. We also go about, and no one has ever mentioned potential riots in Guyana.'

'Is my world the same as yours? The communities I visit only discuss a looming riot,' Rehman says in self-defense.

'Your circle aligns with Cheddi Jagan,' Reeta remarks casually. 'He recently acquired an apprehensive mindset. Guyana trusted him as the leader of the people of its six races. Cheddi remained in power for a decade, promising "We would reduce collectively economic disparity between all six races." Janet advanced programmes of primary schooling, maternal care and rural health centres for people all over the country.'

'You are correct, Reeta. Jagan is the Icon of Unity in Guyana.' Rehman asserts.

'It seems that Uncle Cheddi has overlooked his unique strength of unifying Guyana for the December election. The election slogan of the PPP is *apni jaat, apni* vote. How funny! Cheddi Jagan now aspires to be a leader exclusively for the Indians! Why wouldn't the Afro-Guyanese be skeptical? And why should the Chinese accept a changed Cheddi?'

'The opposition parties are falsely claiming that we Indians had been reaping the rewards, largely benefitting our own community,' Rehman retorts.

'Perhaps there is a salt of truth in their claims. We should re-check our own records over the past decade. If the allegations of the Opposition prove correct, we should admit our failure and extend our apologies!'

'To whom we should extend our apologies, Reeta? To the PNC? To the UF?'

'We owe our apologies not to the political parties, but to the people of Guyana, the voters. If we have shattered their dreams over past eleven years, irrespective of colour and creed, we ought to express our regrets and admit our past failures. If we are sincere with our apologies, Guyana shall vote for us again in 1964,' Reeta advises her father.

Rehman Majeed is taken aback.

'Have you also teamed up with the cause of *Dusree Jaat*, Reeta? Your words sound adversarial. Can't you perceive their oppression and animosity towards the Indian community? We were even denied our basic right to eat rice! They opposed the British providing meagre rice to us. It took seventy years after our arrival in Guyana for rice cultivation to commence, and only then did we have the privilege of enjoying rice on our clay plates.'

'It all happened in the past, Baba! Why dwell on it now? Why cling to a negative notion the authenticity of which could be questioned by modern historians? Let's share what we have today. Yes, historical wrongs were perhaps done to Indians during the eighteenth century, but why would Cheddi Jagan seek revenge during twentieth century?'

'Cheddi is not seeking a revenge. It is a propaganda of the British and American agents. They have infiltrated the media. In fact, in his pre-election speech, Cheddi declared that we, the unified Guyanese, must plan for our future together. Otherwise, there will be peril. We, the Guyanese, ought not align ourselves with the colonial powers. The British is conspiring to delay Guyana's freedom by raising the so-called communist slogan, the so-called red menace. Dusree jaat is not listening to him, for their own races for power, they are aligning with British. They forgot that the PPP have pioneered the freedom movement and made sacrifices for freedom. But they do not trust the PPP anymore!'

'Guyana had trusted the PPP in the past. The Blacks and the Portuguese have voted for the PPP, making it the singular majority party in Guyana. Ask yourself, Baba, how and why have we lost that trust?'

Rehman looks at her, finding Reeta to be a strange girl. When did she start pondering over political matters? When did she shift her thoughts from lipsticks and bangles to cultivating such a political acumen?

'Did you come to discuss politics with me, or do you have other words?' Rehman gently presses her.

'Let's postpone it for now, Baba; I'll share with you another day,' Reeta abruptly changes her tone.

'Come on, dear, you can tell me now. I don't want to be left in suspense,' Rehman urges her affectionately.

'I am idling and waiting at home all day, Baba. When I go to the Bishop's College, I do not enjoy studying, as I used to before my marriage! My classmates cast curious glances at me only because I am a married student. It is a strange feeling! I am unable to concentrate on academic studies. I find myself bored being alone at home. I wish to work outside and earn a living! Could you help me secure a job?'

'Why do you ask for a job, sweetheart? What are you lacking? Mohon's income is substantial. Our business, by the Grace of Allah, is thriving.'

'I don't seek Mohon's financial support. I aspire to stand on my own feet, Baba.'

'What is Mohon's point of view on this?'

'I haven't inquired, Baba. Even if Mohon raises his objections for my professional career, I wouldn't be deterred.'

'With your qualifications, the available jobs will allow a meagre salary. It would not commensurate with the prestige of Majeed family. I suggest you to volunteer with Janet's organisation for development of women cooperatives which helps all the six races. You may find satisfaction with that type of social involvement. Moreover, your Baba is still alive. I am here! Our financial resources would be sufficient to support you.'

'I understand, Baba. I trust your financial stability. I understand I have a rightful claim to it. Nevertheless, I want to ascertain myself, if a situation arises where I need to part ways with Mohon, whether I would be capable to sustain myself, given that empowerment.'

Reeta speaks softly, searching her father's eyes for self-affirmation. Rehman understands her silent urge. He extends his both hands and hugs his distraught daughter, planting a soft kiss on her forehead. Reeta steps away shyly, rubbing her moist eyes.

***

Puzzled by Reeta's words, Rehman repeatedly looks left and right for Paromita. Usually, each morning Paromita waits at the door side, offers a silent prayer for Rehman and hands over a flask filled with his favorite *elaichi* (cardamom) tea with milk and sugar boiled slowly overnight, and a tiffin box containing *Aloo Paratha* and *Roti* which serves both as breakfast and lunch.

Paromita rushes in through the door.

'Rehman, I had to spend a little longer time for my morning prayers! Do you have to go for work so early this morning? I had been having *kudu daak* (dark thoughts) all night and even during the prayer.'

Rehman smiles, 'Do not worry unnecessarily, dear Paromita. The city is calm. The Governor has alerted forces in case riots and arsons surges suddenly. Cheddi holds firm control on the administration and police. Nothing will happen in Georgetown. Moreover, to observe the elections, hundreds of visitors and prospective investors are descending on Guyana. They need car and related services. I have to go to the depot, Paromita.'

'Be careful on the roads. Since the happenings of Black Friday, I am really nervous with my own people.'

'The Black Friday of 1962 will never visit us again. We are brothers, Paromita. Shovon's words have convinced me that the youths of Guyana long for a united nation of six races. No brother will betray the other brother. The British and American agents are spreading false rumours. Please don't pay attention to those gossips.'

'I can see Guyana is divided. People of Guyana do not blindly trust each other anymore!'

'You should not attend the pre-election meetings of the PPP. Perhaps the fear that violent politics will recur is overwhelming for you!' advises Rehman. 'Perhaps you should stay at home for a few days.'

'I am really worried. I am disturbed, Rehman. Mohon left early morning for his routine flights. These days, Mohon is keeping longer at his work. He also looks grumpy all the time.'

Rehman looks at his watch repeatedly.

'Anyway be careful. Please return home early. I feel like cooking something for the family today!'

'How about *Khichuri?*' Rehman steps out while praying the verse of Kursi.

'I will prepare Khichuri on the day of Mawlid and distribute among all my neighbours. Wait for that day!' suggests Paromita with a smile.

***

The long-awaited election takes place on 7 December 1964 without any major incidents of violence. The PPP secures 24 seats with about 46 per cent of the votes. The PNC wins 22 seats with about 41 per cent of votes. The UF wins 7 seats with about 13 per cent of popular votes. Cheddi claims that since the PPP holds single majority in the parliament, it should be invited to form the new government. But the PNC declares that it will strive to align with the UF, enabling them to form a coalition government.

The following evening, Rehman summons Shovon for an urgent consultation. Shovon was returning from his college quite late and seemed tired. They both settle down at the dinner table while Paromita warms up their meal.

'Have you heard the election results?! Cheddi should be invited to form the new government. But, 10, Downing Street is hesitating. Forbes wants power!' says Rehman.

'Baba! At this moment, we aspire freedom from the

colonials! Let Forbes form a new national government.' Shovon unhesitatingly advises. A sense of release envelopes his thoughts.

'I had been in college all day preparing for my final examinations. Despite the day long post-election turmoil, Rania is patiently waiting in her room. I must leave now to join her. We will have dinner together!' Shovon gets up from the table.

'Please wait for the *feerni* (a sweet delicacy made of milk and rice). I have prepared it this morning, specially for you!' Paromita runs to the kitchen to get his favourite dessert.

'I will just sprinkle Gulaab Jal (rose water) for the rose aroma that you like.'

'We are unable to relate with our young generation any longer,' Rehman murmurs to himself. Shovon overhears his Baba and sits back.

'Only because, Baba, your generation is not willing to listen to us. We are distancing ourselves from our parents' generation only because we seek to avert confronting our elders. We respect them for the sacrifices they have made for us, individually and collectively, and for our country. We dare not dishonour the immense sacrifices and economic contributions of our forefathers to our land.'

'I am willing to listen to you, my son. What advise will you offer to me, Shovon?' Rehman softens his voice and strives to bring Shovon nearer to him.

'I will be frank, Baba. My blunt words may again offend you!' Shovon alerts.

'I am listening, Shovon.'

'Cheddi had been Guyana's Premier thrice. During these long periods, Forbes stayed with him steadfast like a younger brother. Let 1964 be Forbes' first turn to lead the nation. Let there be a coalition national government formed by the PPP, PNC and UF.'

'Why should the PPP accept your idea?' asks an amazed Paromita.

'Because we could demand generosity from leadership of the PPP, as a majority party, for our greater good—Guyana's freedom. Forbes holds a global vision. While studying at the London School of Economics, Forbes formed a close rapport with current global leaders such as Kwame Nkrumah, and Abubakar Tafawa Balewa. On the other hand, Cheddi understands the pulse of each of our six races. He is revered equally by the rural and urban populace of Guyana. This will be an exceptionally talented Cabinet. Let Uncle Jagan seize this moment, befool the strategy of our colonial masters of divide and conquer, and deliver the master formula of a national government. We hate the British. The earlier they leave our soil, the better for us.' Shovon looks up straight into his father's eyes.

'Baba, please convey my *salaams* to our Uncles, Sheikh Mohamed Saffee, Abdul Maccie Hamid, Yacoob Ally and

Subhan Ali Ramjohn. They all had been elected from the PPP with overwhelming votes to the Legislature. Also, my salaam to uncle Mohamed Kasim. He had contested under UF banner. Whichever party forms the government, I am confident, we will have a *fullaman* (Muslim man of African descent) in the Cabinet. Afterall, 8 per cent of Guyanese Muslims have secured 10 per cent of the Legislature seats! We fullaman should no longer worry about our visibility in Guyana!' Shovon assures his worried father.

'This is an extra benefit of being a Guyanese Muslim. We can reap the ripe fruits from the top of the tree. And, we are equally equipped to dig out the roots of the rewarding trees,' quips Shovon.

'Before I go upstairs, let me place another challenge for the PPP leadership to ponder, Baba. The British left Jamaica in 1962. Around the same time, they left Trinidad, too. Has the PPP ever thought why those countries gained independence from the British much earlier than us? What factors in Jamaica and Trinidad forced the British into hurried retreats from major economies of the Caribbean? Even more importantly, what social factors of Guyana convinced the British that they could extend their unwanted rule in Guyana for so long? Was it because our octogenarian leadership was shortsighted and divisive? Or, was it because, we, the youth of Guyana, have refrained from actively harnessing our rightful say on the future of our motherland? Many questions are wrestling in our minds. We need to meet in an open forum to sort out and resolve our existing generation gaps together!' exclaims Shovon.

***

'Is my happiness like a Cereus flower—fragile, ephemeral, and unfulfilled?' Reeta ponders poignantly.

The Cereus, an exquisite flower in Guyana, carries a charm as smooth as white wax. However, its fragility is more meaningful than its beauty.

'Shall I too, like the Cereus, fade away with the first light of dawn? I find myself anticipating nothing but neglect. While Rania exudes confidence in her unrestricted passage of youth, I question what to expect from a marriage that feels unwelcomed.'

Reeta sinks into introspection. The Cereus, every young woman in Guyana passionately anticipates touching the Cereus, even if only once, to experience the pure innocence of the flower, before reaching the turbulent years of her youth. They yearn to witness its bloom in the candlelight, to touch and feel its smoothness, to bring their faces close and whisper, 'Don't let my happiness be as short-lived as you, dear Cereus; let my life be abundant in your selfless giving.'

The white, pure, wax-smooth Cereus blooms only once at midnight. However, as soon as the sun's first rays touch its petals, it succumbs to the sun's embrace, offering its own life in exchange for the happiness of another beautiful woman of Guyana. The proud beauties of Guyana await the midnight touch of the Cereus to fulfill their dreams.

Have Reeta's prayers been in vain? It seems that Mohon Singh finds no more allure in Reeta simply because she wears a green diamond wedding ring. Shall her youth evaporate before she had been touched by a man! Why is Mohon oblivious to the intense desire resonating within the fervour of her whole being?

Reeta continues to brood over this all day long, furrowing her brows. She recalls the day Mohon had a first quarrel with her, tossing the pots and pans into the balcony, sleeping in a separate room in enrage, and never returning to their bedroom. He cozied up on the sofa, his solid frame finding a peaceful rest. Was it a comfortable sleep? Reeta yearned during those quiet hours! She would restlessly wake up, yearning to make a trip to Mohon, and playfully stroke his ears with gentle touches and tickles.

Reeta got out of bed and stood at the door, looking a little hesitant. Wearing her black nightgown, a little unkempt, she yearned to comb his shaggy, pitch-dark, rough hair with her fingers and savour the distinctive odour of Mohon's dark body. She felt compelled to bring her slender body nearer, and to shove her soft tender lips against the sleepy Mohon. Should she join him? Could this advance diminish her in the eyes of the obstinate

Mohon? Would she let her bangles chime?

She hoped Mohon would wake up and plead with her to give herself selflessly, as the lovely Cereus does to the blazing rays of the sun? Mohon, the mighty man, would press his sturdy body against hers, crushing her in the pain of satisfaction! Reeta shall immerse herself in a blissful bath for a promising beginning!

Nonetheless, the one who sleeps in pretense does not wake up usually. Reeta quietly returns to her bed, deep in contemplation.

***

Cheddi convenes an anxiously-awaited policy-making meeting of the party leaders together with 24 elected members of the Legislature from the PPP on 10 December 1964.

'The rumours are true. Britain's ruling political elite seeks Cheddi's ouster!' confirmed Ranji Chandisingh, a graduate of Harvard University. 'The British Prime Minister has already sent the Order in Council to the Queen. If the Queen signs it, Cheddi will be deposed. He would no longer be the Prime Minister,' he noted with firm affirmation.

'If that happens, we shall initiate a nationwide movement. Do the British believe Guyana is still enslaved? Will they depose their elected Prime Minister with majority of seats whenever they choose to do so? The Guyanese mass will arise. We shall collectively confront this injustice. Georgetown's protests will intensify dramatically,' Brindley Benn, another newly elected MP declares emphatically.

'This will only exacerbate lawlessness,' Chunilall Josan, an elderly MP responds with cautious concern.

'Burnham is poised to assume the role of Premier at any moment. He claims to command the confidence of the majority of the Legislature. He is not alone. British soldiers from the Naval Force shall accompany him. Any attempt by the PPP to initiate a riot will result in a catastrophe,' cautions Yacoob Ally, a senior elected MP.

'Our cadre is resolute. They will not retreat. I will instigate a non-cooperation movement,' Brindley Benn retorts defiantly.

'Racial hatred already prevails in each and every corner of Guyana. What more do you aim to achieve? Has our appetite for racial conflicts not yet been fully satiated?' Reepu Daman Persaud retorts.

'We shall roll on. We will establish a government of the people led by Cheddi. Burnham has turned into an American puppet. We will dismantle him,' Abdul Maccie Hamid, a dedicated younger elected member, asserted with a firm determination to move ahead with the protest movement. Six others joined him.

Cheddi Jagan had listened so long with patience.

Depressed and bored, he kept his thoughts to himself; but the words of the elder elected MPs lifted his disdain sharply.

'What is this "government of the people" you are talking about? You have lost power yourselves by alienating your party from its grassroot supports. I am reminded of a saying by Chinese Comrade Mao Tse Tung. Speaking against dogmatism during the Civil War in the post-thirties, he said, those now in power, you no longer have the ability to topple them. You cannot overthrow them. As a result, you overthrow those who are not in power. Those who are helpless, vulnerable, or destitute. Those who want daily necessities from you, and not political power! During your past parliamentary tenure, you did not strive to meet their expectations; you rarely visited your constituency. You never strive to meet the basic daily needs of your rural voters, yet you blame your grassroots voters! Bharat, in the name of the people's government, you have brought about your own doom.'

'No, Cheddi, you have failed yourself. You have brought about your own defeat,' Moses Bhagwan, an aged leader, gave Cheddi Jagan a hard, pointed look.

Cheddi Jagan looked back at him, emitting a confidence never witnessed before by the party members. Cheddi declared, 'No, Bhagwan. I'm not exhausted yet. I have seen kings fall and queens lose their kingdoms. I will live on! I will live to see Burnham and his puppet government wither away, slowly and over time.'

'No, Cheddi Jagan, you will only live to see your own downfall! That fall is coming. It's imminent,' Ranji Chandisingh, perhaps the oldest MP, stared at Cheddi with his bright eyes radiating a strange strong rebuke.

***

Following the elections, the art exhibition had to be extended by another seven days. The entire Guyana seemed to be converging to witness the art exhibition, an unprecedented event in the country's history. Visitors flocked from distant places like Essequibo, Port Mourant, Enmore, and Far Portico. However, Reeta showed no interest in attending. She sat at home, indifferent, casting vacant looks at the azure sky. Occasionally, her gaze shifted to the neatly arranged pictures of her wedding on the dressing table. Reeta considered herself genuinely attractive—with a smile on her lips, a shy gleam in her eyes, and a sharp nose. Yet, she remained undesirable to Mohon Singh.

Reeta throws a sharp glance at Mohon. He is sleeping on the sofa until late this morning. Has his morning flight been cancelled? He returned about midnight. Reeta wonders, why does Mohon Singh get shaken in Reeta's presence? He gazes at her like an entranced earthworm, captivated, yet motionless. No hand is raised, no call is made, and no advantage is taken, though it is rightfully his. Instead, he hides, retreats, and withdraws, suspicion emanating from his eyes like a dark light.

Reeta scrutinises Mohon, a strong, vigorous young man. The Roman physique gracing his tall and erect figure could ignite the desire of any young woman with excitement, leading to absolute destiny. Yet, there is one flaw in Mohon Singh—his body is dark, deep dark, a curious blend of African and Indian features, perhaps rendering a Roman physique lovable and attractive! Reeta's fury surges. Her maa had arranged this marriage without her consent, and though she did not fall in love with Mohon, she obediently accepted the union as a symbol of her supposedly blissful life. However, her mother overlooked Mohon's evident flaws.

In Guyanese Indian society, colour preference is astonishingly intense. Fairness is coveted not only for girls, but also for boys. The fairer the complexion, the higher the chances of success and societal approval. Black, despite any claims of shaded skins, is met with disdain in people's eyes. Indian men with darker skins face similar challenges in the marital race. Compared to Mohon, Reeta is not only blessed with fair skin but also radiates like a rosy Portuguese girl. Mohon Singh is absolutely incompatible with Reeta, and, as people gaze upon them at bazaar, some even smile or wince expressing their disapproval. They have disgust in their eyes as they question the taste that led this Indian paragon of beauty to choose a man like Mohon.

Reeta, as she contemplates attending the art exhibition, directs her anger towards Paromita for not recognising Mohon's shortcomings. After all, she is her own mother. She could have appreciated the secret dreams of her beautiful girl.

Reeta steps out, adorning her latest bell-bottoms imported from Trinidad and black goggles, ready to check the displayed artwork on the last few days of the exhibition. She wonders if the art could surpass her radiance.

Reeta meticulously examines each of the ninety-seven pictures. Some depict rough sea views, flighty birds, bustling markets, and tired families. There are images of sports-playing children and the cries of newborns, reflecting the diversity of human experiences.

Reeta, uninterested, blinks lightly, standing still for a moment. She notices that paintings of beautiful women are displayed as scattered images throughout the exhibition hall, totalling around fifteen to twenty. Each of these paintings features a nude woman. Reeta waits directly in front of each painting. Standing erect, she examines each artwork with a surgeon's precision, mentally surveying the various body parts of the model and her expressions. She observes seven to nine different models of different ages, teenagers, young adults, and young women, had been captured each in a distinct posture. Some models exhibit happiness, while others display pain or weariness. Reeta is impressed by the artist's talent. After all, fine arts was her favourite subject at Bishop's College. She notices how each model had an amazing ability to convey distinctive emotions through her bare physique.

Reeta wonders if all the paintings are the work of the same artist, recognising a consistent style in tension and colour usage. Walking towards an image, she struggles to figure out the artist's name, finding it intricately written.

'You must study it carefully! The artist's name is Camacho,' Rodriguez steps forward, positioning himself beside Reeta. He had been observing her for quite a while. Even though she had been at the exhibition for two hours, her attention was solely on the representations of beautiful women. Among the diverse array of girls from Guyana at the art fair, he felt that the beauty of this particular lady surpassed all others.

Reeta turns around and spots Rodriguez.

'Thank you. The name was difficult to read. The writing is quite intricate,' Reeta remarks.

'I believe you enjoyed our art exhibition so far!' Rodriguez insinuates.

'Artist of each painting is amazingly talented. Each painting exudes a remarkable, lifelike quality. I can't help but suspect they all share the touch of a same skilled artist,' Reeta observes with the tone of a seasoned art critic.

'You've got it right,' Rodriguez says, returning the compliment with a smile. 'You have a keen artistic sense. All the women were, indeed, painted by the same artist.'

'There's a poetic quality to the artist's mind, expressed in his art. The models seem alive, like a poem that needs to be recited only when rays of the afternoon sun start setting. Cooler rays invite us to explore further through our deep vivid eyes. Our eyes should stare directly into the sparkling eyes of each model for hearing silent whispers of her own story!' Reeta expresses dreamily.

'I hope I'm not sharing unnecessary ramblings with another art gallery visitor. I'm Reeta,' her normal composure returns.

'I curated this exhibition,' replies Rodriguez.

'Nice knowing you!' Reeta folds her hands into a namaskar.

'Could you please convey my respect and heartfelt congratulations to the artist? I'm truly impressed by his drawing abilities,' Reeta says with deep admiration.

'I humbly accept your compliments. My long artist life feels worthwhile this afternoon,' Rodriguez nods.

Reeta appears thrilled.

'My other name is Camacho; full name is Camacho Rodriguez. Today, my drawing is, indeed, worthwhile.'

Rodriguez bows and kisses Reeta's finally outstretched hand in a French manner.

They sit for tea at the coffee lounge of Clara Lodge—Rodriguez and Reeta.

Next to the small table, near the window, is a planter where the bloomed red Sharon of Roses are casting shifting shadows directly on Reeta's face. She notices a Tityra, trotting at the lawn for food, staring at her with frequent glances of wonder.

'Is painting your sole profession, or does your family take up your time?' Reeta with a playful smile, asks.

'My artistic life provides me with my simple daily necessities. Though I'm not rich, I can find joy in the laughter of my friends. I indulge in a drink now and then. I can afford a good steak. And, on occasions, I am able to make a trip to the cinema,' Rodriguez chuckles.

'Where do you find your models for the paintings? Do they all know you, or are they strangers? Sweethearts, perhaps?' curious, Reeta inquires while sipping her special expresso coffee.

'No, each of them appeared in my life like flashes of light, and transformed themselves into an invaluable moment in the simple life of this painter. During my journey, I keep my eyes open,' admits Rodriguez.

'Sometimes, it happens spontaneously. Some are familiar faces, while others are strangers. Maybe they catch my eyes unexpectedly with their striking beauty. That's when I approach them, expressing my desire to draw them.'

'And do they agree?' Reeta probes.

'Not everyone agrees. Some decline politely. I appreciate their candid words. I retreat,' admits Rodriguez. 'But I am not usually rejected. A few invitees accepted my invitation outright; while a few models waited for a while before returning, expressing their interest.'

'Which means, you indeed keep track of your prospective models?' Reeta speaks with an alluring smile.

'Perhaps they realised that my door is always open to redeem the offer!' Rodriguez conveys with a deep philosophical stare.

Reeta senses something churning within Rodriguez's mind.

'For instance, I would love to draw you right now. Would you be willing?' Rodriguez looks at Reeta directly with throbbing anticipation.

Reeta notices a peculiar fascination in Rodriguez's eyes—the fervent urge of an artist for creating an immortal artwork for a global audience.

'I don't mind being drawn,' she whispers slowly. Rodriguez smiles and says with a hesitant caution, 'I paint nothing, but nudes.'

Reeta remains silent. The alluring Reeta is ready to become extraordinary in the eyes of the artist tonight.

***

Frequent knocks echo on Rodriguez's door. Impatient taps. Rodriguez is taking a shower. Soap lathers his body, creating a foamy silhouette. Hearing the knocks, Reeta glances back. Is it time for someone to arrive, or is someone about to arrive? Reeta is startled, wrapping her wet towel more tightly.

'I asked for room service to deliver dinner,' Rodriguez explains, his voice melting as the shower flows.

Another loud, insistent bang on the door irritates Rodriguez.

'Well, the room service boy has no patience. A complaint should be lodged.' Rodriguez turns off the shower.

'Reeta, please unlock the door. Let him deliver the dinner. You must be very hungry. And keep the receipt. I'll sign it later,' he instructs while drying his body with a white towel.

Another loud knock reveals the impatience of the person outside.

Reeta tightly secures her towel, removes the door chain, turns the knob and opens the door partly.

A worried Rehman Majeed pushes the door open and enters forcefully.

'The Queen has just signed an Order in Council. Cheddi Jagan has been deposed. The Governor invited Forbes Burnham to swear in as Prime Minister. The BBC World has just reported,' Rehman shouts.

Rehman spouts breathlessly. But his words remain incomplete.

A scared Reeta shaking behind the open door stood next to her charcoal-sketched drawing etched on the erect canvas.

A silent Rehman stumbles out of the room.

Reeta keeps her trembling eyes focused on the front wall. A wall calendar is hanging from a hook. The ceiling fan is on the high cycle. The pages of the calendar are flipping by the whirling wind. Reeta notices the date, 12 December 1964.

Reeta realises that birth, marriage and death are indeed destined.

Rehman Majeed slowly walks towards the seawall. He shakily holds in his left hand his prayer mat smeared by his sweat. He lays the smelly mat and faces the *qibla*. The waves of the Atlantic Sea are hitting the Seawall of Georgetown with a huge roar. The sun is setting. The time of Maghrib prayer sets in.

Standing on the prayer mat, Rehman commences his routine evening prayer to his Lord. He fulfills the rituals of the prayers. He turns his face to the right and offers his salaam to the awaiting unseen angels and to citizens sitting or walking beside him. Similarly, he turns his face to the left and expresses his salaam, 'May the peace of Allah be with you,' to the awaiting unseen angels and to passersby walking down the seawall. He raises his both hands towards the blue sky of Guyana and addresses his Lord:

'Oh Allah, Indians have built the Taj Mahal, a timeless symbol of love. We Guyanese have built this seawall to fend off rough waves of the Atlantic Sea. We constructed it with the labour of thousands of citizens, those who were indigenous to this land and those migrating from distant lands of Africa, Asia and South America. We have settled ourselves in this land. We have staked the future of our generations by embracing this land as our own, for all our six races. But at what costs? Just to turn into an icon of deceit between the races? Within the white marble of the Taj Mahal, I couldn't find the essence of a pure mind. A history of atrocities is concealed within Taj Mahal. But the red pebbles of the seawall are a reflection of the determination of six races marching hand in hand towards freedom. We sought freedom collectively and individually. We promised to break the shackles of our impoverished mind. But would the impending freedom will carry the signature of stigma, doubts and betrayal for our progenies?'

The faded rays of the setting sun, mixed with the looming darkness of the evening, were reflecting on the stormy waves of the sea. The vibrant hues of the setting rays danced on the turbulent waves, casting a colourful glow. Rehman Majeed turns his eyes towards the sinking rays, resembling thundering iron, as if an unknown blacksmith had just forged it with a resounding bang. The light bathes the entire seawall, spreading waves of heat like flames. Rehman feels the fiery resonance of a dreamy blacksmith, as if the irons were encircling him, growing thicker and thicker.

He keeps his hands raised in prayer.

'I was a grocer, and later I became a chauffeur of a

rental car. I stayed a chauffeur! I earned money through hard work. I worked hard. I built my houses with my labour. I did honest business. I raised children. I taught them in the best schools to acquire the knowledge that you have bestowed to the global humanity.

'Tell me, Allah, why should I still seek to stay on this earth? Why should I live further? My son, fully entitled to his youth, is enjoying his life to the maximum. My daughter proudly searches for her soul in a stranger's hotel room. Ensnared in the whirlpool of Machiavellian politics, my wife drifts, captivated by the influence of the astute politics of rival politicians. Sometimes on this side, sometimes on the other, like a rat caught in a cage. My longtime friend does not hesitate to compromise friendship in search of beautiful models. My leader, in his lust for power, triggers his own downfall by making false choices. Allah, tell me, how do I continue to live among them?'

Rehman brings his hands together, continuing his prayer.

'Allah, do me just one more favour: Please, enable me to internalise your dictate for submission. Guide me to its meaning before the call of my return to you commences. I am waiting! Let me understand the eternal truth.'

Rehman Majeed touches his brow, then his cheek, and brings his hands down, finishing the prayer.

'Oh Allah! My aged generation has failed to unify our

six races. But our next young generation realises the need of unifying the people of Guyana under a free nation. Please, expedite our freedom and enable the progenies of our six races to live together, till the eternity, in our promised motherland.'

Rehman opens his weeping eyes. The fading rays of the settled sun gently touch his outstretched hands. It promises the Sun shall rise, again and again, on the promised land of Guyana.

Rehman again bows down, letting his forehead touch the soil of his own land. The feeling of mother is remarkably assuring. Rehman bows his forehead again to his own soil.

Acknowledgements

Rhythms of Resistance is a work of fiction anchored in the layered history of indentured workers and slaves traded over three centuries. It was originally published in 1987 in Bengali as *Pegasus,* dwelling on the legacy of indentured workers at the Caribbeans. Subsequently, *Pegasus* drew the attention of readers with several editions.

I extend my deep gratitude to my lifelong friend, Fakhruzzaman Chowdhury (late), for his invaluable support in bringing this story to life, and to Qayyum Chowdhury (late), a legend of fine arts in Bangladesh, who has designed the cover page and the internal sketches of the Bengali edition of *Pegasus.*

After 37 years of the first publication of *Pegasus* in Bangladesh, Faruq Ahmed, a recognised poet and journalist, suggested placing the novel on a global platform with a rendering in English. A dedicated team—comprising Milton Mollah, an accomplished writer; Nausheen Noor, former Lifestyle Editor of *Harper's Bazaar* and contributor of *Vogue Arabia* and Vichitra Goel, a proficient editor and literary representative—collaborated with me with exceptional diligence and enthusiasm to curate this English version. Atiqur Rahman, a recognised artist from Dhaka, helped me with the graphics.

I am grateful to Dr Richard Cambridge, Ms Zena John, and Shuja Nawaz, my colleagues at The World Bank, for their valuable insights. I also sought the guidance of Fayezul Chowdhury and Yasmeen Chowdhury, connoisseurs of culture and literature, whose wisdom and constructive advises have further enriched my work. I extend my sincere appreciation to Renu K Verma, Managing Director of Vitasta Publishing, for inviting me to join Vitasta's family of Authors.

I wish to express my appreciation to Waseem Noor, Wameek Noor, Klaus Kajer, Prithvi Rajkumar, and Sumitra Rajkumar, who patiently listened to my incessant tales of Guyana.

Finally, I acknowledge my debt to Najma Noor for lending me time for my lifelong writings.

I hope *Rhythms of Resistance* would be well received by the English-speaking readers around the world.

About the Author

Dr Abdun Noor's professional career spanned over 45 years (1970–2015) at The World Bank at Washington DC. He focused on formulation of institutional policies for education and human resource development outlining how financing for the education sector by The World Bank shall assist the poorest of the poor, enhance adult literacy and expedite universal primary education for the developing countries. After the emergence of Bangladesh as an independent country, Dr Abdun Noor, led the formulation of the Education and Manpower Policies for First Five Year Development Plan (1974-1978), prepared by Bangladesh Planning Commission.

Abdun Noor pursued his literary career from student life. During college days of 1950s, he wrote prolifically for children and young readers. The 1960s saw him delve into writing short stories for the literary magazines and broadcast media. His first play, *Eclipsed Sun*, was staged at prestigious Curzon Hall of Dhaka University during the 1960s. But his passion for writing plays flourished over succeeding years with over twenty plays broadcasted over national radio and television channels some of which are still available on YouTube (eg *Char Dayal*). In 1999, his play *The Quest* was staged in English in Washington, DC.

Abdun Noor wrote five novels dwelling on the global values of basic human rights and emancipation of the disadvantaged. *Tetallish Siri* (43 steps), his first novel dwells on the urbanisation process of affluent rural societies by gradual induction to flat based colonies (1964). *Pegasus,* set in 1964 depicts the spirit of six races of British Guinea for freedom (1987). *Shunyabritto* (An Empty Circle) explores the odyssey of immigrants from Bangladesh on pursuit of American Dream (1993) *Uttaran* (Overcoming) portrays the craving of a married woman for a child shackled under traditional values of the society during the age of globalisation (2004). *Bicholito Somoy* (An Uncertain Time) a two-volume epic set-in 17th-century Mughal-occupied Bangla and Assam, highlights the resilience of the citizen and society against exploitation of colonial European traders (2005, 2007) and was recognised as the best fiction publication of 2005.

Dr Abdun Noor's latest publication in English, *Thy Names,* elaborates the 99 qualities of One God, *Asmaa-ul-Husna* of Islamic faith, as an endeavour for an inter-faith journey to spirituality (2016).

Dr Abdun Noor, is recipient of lifetime achievement award for creative writings from several international literary platforms such as: Second DC Boi Mela (Washington DC, 2023), First NRB/ PBO Literature and Culture Conference (Dhaka, 2024), 34th New York International Bangla Boimela (Jamaica, 2025).

Dr Abdun Noor, a US citizen, lives in Bethesda, Maryland.

Email: abdunnoor0202@gmail.com